THE
BASTARD

THE FILTHY TRILOGY BOOK ONE

NEW YORK TIMES BESTSELLING AUTHOR
LISA RENEE
JONES

ISBN-13: 978-1731114464

To obtain permission to excerpt portions of the text, please contact the author at lisareneejones.com/contact.

All characters in this book are fiction and figments of the author's imagination.

www.lisareneejones.com

CHAPTER ONE

Eric

When the Kingston family decides to throw a party, it means no less than two hundred people at their twenty-thousand-foot Aspen estate, valets at the door, an abundance of Kingston Motors luxury cars in the drive, and money. Lots of money, because Jeff Kingston has nothing to do with anyone who doesn't have money, aside from me, his bastard son, otherwise known as the backup heir just in case my half-brother kicks the bucket.

I exit the guest house, where I'm staying until my meeting with my father tomorrow, which I shouldn't have accepted. I don't know why the fuck I'm even here, aside from the fact that these people are supposed to be my people, and leaving the SEALs was like leaving family. It's hard to let go of that need for a family unit. Family. Right. What the hell was I thinking? Like I could ever really be a Kingston.

I walk down a stone path shrouded in flowers and low hanging trees, twisting left and then right until I enter the courtyard filled with bodies in fancy dresses and tuxedos like the one I'm in now. A waiter walks by and I snag a glass of champagne when I'd rather have whiskey, but I'll settle for anything to get me through tonight's launch of a new model of car. I barely give a shit about the old model, which is exactly why my father shouldn't want me to work for him. I walk to one of the few dozen standing tables covered in white tablecloths, down my drink and accept another when my gaze catches on a woman, on *her* and *just her*.

She's standing on the other side of the pool, a princess in a strappy black dress, with flawless skin and long brown hair,

1

surrounded by her subjects. At least, that's how she reads to me, no doubt like every other socialite I've ever met in this godforsaken world, and yet I'm watching her when I never watch them. There's something about this woman, a white swan among the black swans on a pond made of money and death, my mother's death most specifically, since that's how I got here.

My princess must feel my attention because she tunes out the conversation she's having with several other people, her chin lifting, her gaze sweeping wide and then catching mine. I don't even think about looking away. I don't care that she knows that I'm watching her. I don't care if she knows that I'm thinking about fucking her. I'm the bastard in these parts. From the time I was thrust into this place right before my senior year of high school, I do what I do and everyone whispers about it. I'm not going to change that now. Let them whisper about what I want, and this woman, whoever the fuck she is, is worth the whispers.

The man next to her touches her elbow, his gaze shooting in my direction, his jaw setting hard with anger. Priceless and so typical of my father's class of people. He's pissed at me for getting his woman's attention. He should have fucked her better. My cellphone buzzes with a text message and I cut my stare, downing my champagne and then reaching for my phone to find a message from Grayson Bennett, a close friend from my first go at Harvard right before I left and went into the Navy. He's not a bastard, but rather the true heir to the Bennett empire.

Call me, his message says, which is typical Grayson. He wants something, he asks, and usually with actual words. And since we have unfinished business I don't want overheard, I walk toward the house where I know I can find that whiskey. I'll likely find the rightful heir to the throne, right along with our father as well, but at least I'll make my showing and get the hell out of here.

"There he is. My brother."

My jaw clenches at the sound of Isaac's voice even before he steps into my path, and as if for the first time ever he knows what I want, and cares, he offers me one of the two

2

whiskey glasses in hand. "The good stuff. The kind we drink around these parts."

He doesn't mean we, as in me and him, he means we as in the Kingston family, which I've never been a part of. Our eyes lock and hold, the drama of the past, the hatred between us, and I have no doubt the crackle of energy around us is the attention of the room. We are after all the heir and would-be heir who hate each other. Him the prince, with thick, dark hair and green eyes, while I'm simply the bastard, with wavy brown hair, blue eyes, and a good four inches on Isaac at my height of six-foot-two. I don't look like I'm his blood. I damn sure don't feel like his blood, but my mother made sure I can't be denied. She took the damn DNA test that changed my life and not for the better in my opinion.

I accept the glass and his gaze goes to the ink peeking from beneath my white shirt, and lingers on the Rolex on my wrist, before lifting. "Looks like someone got all inked up."

"The bastard brother might as well look the role, right?"

"You're never going to let me live down calling you that, now are you?"

"You don't need to live it down, Isaac, but you will have to face me every day if I decide to join the company, and we both know that didn't go well for you at Harvard."

His eyes spark with a familiar anger I don't have to intentionally stir. He hates me for being the bastard child of his father's mistress, the brother thrust on him only months after his mother died. An ironic turn of events considering my mother's cancer. He steps closer, toe to toe, all up close and friendly. "If you think that because you're some sort of SEAL Team Six hero or something, that I won't buckle you right at the knees, you're wrong. You will not take what is mine."

"I see you two got right back into the brotherly love."

At the sound of my father's voice, Isaac grimaces and my lips quirk. "Seems we have," I say, as Isaac rotates and we both face my father, who looks fit and younger than his fifty-four years in his tuxedo with his dark hair. "I have someone I want you to meet," he says, and The Princess steps to his side, her crystal blue eyes meeting mine as my father says, "Eric. Meet your stepsister, Harper."

CHAPTER TWO

Eric

Harper steps in front of me and Isaac and I offer her my hand. "Nice to meet you, Harper," I say, and when our eyes meet at this close proximity, the spark between us is so damn combustible there's no way it goes unnoticed.

She presses her palm to mine, her gaze dropping to a portion of my inked arm to the collection of colors and designs that make up my full sleeve and reflect everything and somehow nothing in my life. Her lips part, her expression intrigued by the design, not at all the disgust I expect from a perfect princess. She tightens her grip on mine ever-so-slightly and looks up at me. "Nice to *finally* meet you," she says, and fuck, the raspy quality to her voice makes my cock twitch.

"Finally?" I ask, arching a brow and forcing myself to release her.

"Harper's become quite the protégé the past year," my father says. "You'd think she was blood like you two, but then, her father owned a competing business we've now absorbed."

"I was with him night and day," Harper says. "I learned a lot from him at a young age."

She's my father's protégé and if she didn't want to fuck me as badly as I want to fuck her, she'd probably want to fuck me right out of town. Yet another priceless moment. "I need to make a phone call," I say, and I don't wait for anyone's permission.

I down the whiskey Isaac handed me, set down the glass, and step around Harper, my destination once again the castle-like house that is the centerpiece of the property. No one stops me. No one welcomes me because this isn't home for me and they know it. If this trip has done one thing for me, it's to remind me that I'm not in the midst of the Grayson Bennett clan, and a family that takes care of each other and wins together. These are the Kingstons, one step up from the devil's own family.

I reach my destination and enter the back door, directly into the kitchen which is the size of the mobile home I grew up in with my mother, right up until the time she killed herself before the cancer took her. Of course, she didn't leave me in that trailer. She spent her dying days proving that I was the bastard child of Jeff Kingston and forcing him to claim me. I walk through the archway and down a hallway to the right toward my father's office, which is where I'll find whiskey a few grades higher than the bullshit Isaac gave me like I wouldn't know better.

Once I'm inside the man-cave of an office, with bookshelves lining the walls and a sunken seating area with couches and chairs, I walk to the bar in the corner, pour a thirty-year-old whiskey and sit down in a chair. After a damn good taste, I pull my phone from my pocket and dial Grayson.

"My man," he says. "That stock you hooked me up with came through in a big way. You're a beast. That IQ of yours is financial genius."

That IQ I inherited from a mother who never put hers to use for anything but bad. "Glad it worked out, man. Are we even now?"

"You paid for the past two years at Harvard and then some. I took the extra money and invested it back into the stock, for you."

"Consider it yours. Interest for loaning me the money."

"I don't need the money. I'll reinvest it in you ten times over, but I know you have your own empire to run down there in Colorado."

I down the whiskey and decide I'm done. I'm going to get drunk if I don't slow the fuck down. "I'm the heir bastard, not the heir apparent. You know that."

"I know what you are," Grayson says, "and it's nobody's bastard. You have a place right here by my side, not in some office two buildings over, if you decide you want it. Otherwise, I want a piece of Kingston Motors, if you're running it."

That's not going to happen. The question is, do I want any part of aiding in its success? I must. Why else would I be here? "Orian. Buy big. Buy fast."

"You want in?"

"Yeah. Anything you made for me, put it in."

"You got it. When do you have that meeting with your father?"

"Tomorrow after this godforsaken launch party."

"Call me after it's over. Just remember you owe him nothing. You paid for your own school and you have a brilliant financial mind. He needs you. He knows it. Don't let him convince you it's the opposite."

"Right. I'll call you tomorrow."

We disconnect and I stick my phone back inside my pocket before pulling a mini Rubik's cube from my pocket, rotating the puzzle in my hand, and thinking back to the psychologist who'd placed the first one in my hand. My father had hired him to try to "normalize" my behavior. A savant, the physiologist had said, needs a focal point, a way to slow the data in my head, and he was right.

I scramble and solve the cube three times, settling my mind into a place of reckoning, and then shove the cube back in my pocket. The bottom line: I don't belong here. I never belonged here. I stand up and walk to my father's desk where I sit down and think about those words: *You owe him nothing.*

Not exactly true. My father took me in when my mother died. He petitioned to get me into Harvard based on my academic record, which had been dismissed because of my trailer trash background. I owe him, but I don't want to owe him anything more. I'm not going to work for my father. I'm leaving. I grab a pen and a piece of paper and write a note to my father:

In payment for the whiskey I just drank and the roof over my head. If I were you, I'd invest big in Orian and do it quickly. —Your Bastard Son.

I drop the pen and stand up, walking toward the door, my decision made. I'll stay for the meeting tomorrow, simply because he did give me a roof over my head, even if it was to push Isaac, which meant shoving us at each other like a dog fight on repeat. That's what he wants now, to use me to drive Isaac, but Isaac is vicious and not all that smart. I'll eat Isaac alive. I just don't want to anymore.

I exit to the hallway, and when I look left, Harper is exiting the bathroom. I don't even hesitate. I walk toward her while she freezes in place. I don't stop until I'm standing directly in front of her. She looks up at me, the scent of roses lifting in the air and apparently I like roses a whole hell of a lot more than I thought I did because her scent is driving me wild. I don't know what the hell happens, but my hand slides under her hair, and I lean in, my lips next to her lips.

Her hand settles on my chest and grips my lapel, that perfect mouth of hers tilting toward mine as if she's offering it to me. "What are you doing?" she demands, sounding breathless.

"What does it look like I'm doing? Kissing my *sister*." My mouth slants over hers and my tongue slides right past those perfect lips, and with one deep stroke, she moans, and I'm undone. I don't think I've ever wanted to kiss anyone more than I want to kiss this woman right here, right now. I deepen the kiss and press her against the wall, my free hand at her waist, her hand on my hand. Her tongue meets mine for every lick and stroke until I pull back and stare down at her.

Voices sound nearby and I take that last few minutes and decide to do her a favor and be honest with her, like no one else in my father's world will. "He's using you, just like he's always used me. We're the ones who push Isaac to keep him sharp. You'll never inherit. You'll never be anything but The Princess standing next to your King and brother. And just for the record. I'm not your fucking brother." I release her and

8

walk away, making a fast path through the kitchen and out of the house.

Once I'm in the midst of the crowd, I cut through the mess of people and find my way back to the path to my cottage where I enter and have every intention of packing up and getting the hell out of here. I've barely shut the door when the bell rings. Who the hell followed me to the cottage, because someone sure as fuck did. I fling open the door to find Harper standing there.

"Because why would anyone think that I have anything real to bring to the table, right?" she challenges, as if we were still in the middle of our prior conversation, her beautiful blue eyes sparking with anger. "Because all my time with my father, learning his business, taught me nothing."

I grab her and pull her inside the cottage.

CHAPTER THREE

Eric

In about thirty seconds, I have the door shut and locked, and Harper pressed against the wall, my thighs shackling hers. "You don't get to tell me what I can or cannot do," she hisses, as if she doesn't notice that I'm about double her size and presently the one in control.

"How old are you?" I demand.

"What does that have to do with anything?" she snaps back, not even close to backing down.

"How old?" I repeat.

"Twenty-three, but I still don't get why that has anything to do with this."

"How long have you been out of school?"

"Just because I'm not a thirty-year-old literal genius doesn't mean I have nothing to offer, and the suggestion that it does makes you an asshole."

"I'm not suggesting that you have nothing to offer. I'm telling you it doesn't matter to him. I thought it did, too, way back when. I thought if I was better than Isaac, I'd have a place. It didn't. I won't."

"Then why are you even here?"

"Apparently to kiss you." My fingers tangle in her hair and I lower my mouth to hers.

"This is a bad idea," she whispers, but her voice is raspy, affected, the taste of her hunger damn near on my tongue.

I kiss her, a quick brush of lips, and a lick that has the heat between us damn near explosive. "Still think it's a bad idea?"

Her hands flatten on my chest but they flex rather than push. "We both know this is wrong."

"And yet you followed me here."

"You said that already,"

"You knew what would happen," I accuse.

"I was angry."

I certainly know where anger and family collide, in ways I won't explain to anyone. My jaw sets hard and I release her, putting a wide step between us. "Stay or go, but if you stay, you're going to end up naked."

"I know your father's an asshole, but my mother loves him and my father's company is now a part of this one."

"The part where I said that if you stayed, you'd end up naked." I reach for her and pull her to me. "You did understand that, correct?"

"I don't scare off that easily. If I did, I wouldn't be working for your father and under your brother."

"It's me I want you under," I say, molding her close, my hands sliding up her back.

"I'm too young and stupid for business, but I'm just right to fuck?" she challenges.

"I'm warning you, Harper, not talking down to you. And if you're young and stupid, so was I."

"You wanted to be here," she says, and it's not a question or the accusation I'd get from Isaac.

"Yes," I say, tangling my fingers into her hair. "I wanted to be here, just like I want to be right here, right now, with you." My mouth closes down on hers once more, a deep thrust of tongue that's as unforgiving as my father would be if it came down to choosing her or Isaac. It's all about demand and I expect her to push back, to give me the rejection that sends her to the door and me to the fucking airport. That's not what I get.

Her hand on my chest doesn't push me away. She moans and her elbow softens, those perfect curves I'd admired from a distance now pressed nice and close, right up to the moment she jerks back. "My God. What are we doing? You're my stepbrother."

I walk her back against the wall, my hands caressing up her ribcage to cup her breasts. "I told you," I say, stroking my thumbs over her nipples. "I'm not your fucking brother. Not now. Not ever." I cup her face, lean in and my mouth finds her mouth, and if she thought my tongue unforgiving before now, she was wrong. This is unforgiving. It's in my blood. It's who I am, who I was born to be. A bastard who wants her.

I have this sudden need that consumes me. I shove my hand into the top of her dress, fingering her nipple. She makes this soft, sexy sound that has my cock twitching, expanding beneath my zipper. As if she knows, she presses her hand to my crotch and holy fuck, I need inside this woman. I push off the wall and shrug out of my jacket, my gaze raking over the tops of her breasts. Her teeth scrape her bottom lip, and I want that mouth on my body. I want my mouth on *her* body.

I toss the jacket, rip away my tie, and she doesn't run away as I half expect she will. She closes the space between us, her fingers on my buttons, working them down my shirt, but when one hand slides down to my crotch, I react. I slow things down before I fuck her and this is over, and when it is, I'm gone. Suddenly I'm not ready to leave, which is why I turn her to the wall, and force her hands to its surface, yanking down her zipper before I pull my shirt over my head. I step into her, my erection at her backside, my lips at her ear.

"You saw me watching you across the pool," I say, my fingers catching the straps at her shoulders.

"Of course I saw you. You *wanted* me to see you."

"Yes. I did. I wanted you to know I wanted to fuck you." I shove the straps of her dress down her arms. "I wanted you to know I wanted you naked." I pull the dress down, and with no bra to contend with I have it down her hips and to her feet. I lift her and kick it away, taking a moment to appreciate just how perfect her heart-shaped ass is before I turn her to face me.

My fingers tangle in her hair and I pull her to me. "And since you're here," I add, "I will assume you got that message loud and clear."

"I'm still angry and you're still an arrogant asshole, but apparently it doesn't matter, so fuck me before I come to my senses."

I press my cheek to hers, my hand on her cheek, lips by her ear. "I promise to use my tongue in all the right places to make sure you have no regrets."

She pants out a breath that tells me my words affect her and I'm right there when she does, kissing her again, drinking her in, and damn she tastes good; one part innocence, one part a drug that knows how good it feels. And she does feel so fucking good.

I scoop her up and carry her through the living area to the bedroom, because hell, I don't know, it just feels like I should fuck her on the bed, though I could have easily kept her right there by the door. I want this woman. I want her in a bad way and I wanted her from the moment I saw her by that pool. I set her on her feet and I pull her close. "This is where I lick and you come on my tongue."

CHAPTER FOUR

Eric

I'm about to go down on my knee and make good on that promise to lick Harper to orgasm when she suddenly rejects that idea and me. "No," she whispers, flattening her hands on my chest. "No. This is a mistake. I need to leave."

She tries to pull away but I catch her waist and pull her to me. "What just happened?"

"I don't do this kind of thing, ever. I don't know why I'm half naked with you right now."

"This is why," I say, cupping her head and kissing her, my tongue stroking deep and long, the tension in her body easing almost instantly, a tiny moan sliding from her mouth. "That's why," I repeat, when she's all soft and yielding in my arms. "Because you want me and I want you."

"You want *something*," she accuses as if she's decided I have an agenda I don't have.

"I want you or I'd be gone already," I say, pulling back to let her see the truth in my face. "You're the only reason I'm not driving away right now."

"Because I fit your agenda?"

"My only agenda right now is you on my tongue." I kiss her again. "And what does me between your legs do for me besides turn us both on?"

"I won't be a weapon against them or you."

"I'm fighting a war. I don't need a weapon. Don't make this complicated. Don't make me complicated. I'm here, I'm gone. I want to fuck you before I leave. You want to fuck me, too, and right now, I'm going to kiss you again unless you—"

"Stop talking," she orders fiercely. "Stop and give me time to think. Stop—"

My mouth slants over hers, and the instant my tongue touches hers, she moans and kisses me back, a wild hungry kiss, my hand on her breast, her nipple.

She moans, and God, I love this woman's moans. My cock throbs against my zipper and I need her on my tongue and everywhere I can get her. I lower myself to one knee, my hands on her hips, slipping her panties off. As I look up at her, there's a hint of trepidation in her eyes that I don't want to exist, and I know comes from family, that war that she wrongly believes I'm fighting.

"I'm going to make you forget about everything but fucking," I promise, my lips pressing to her belly, my tongue flicking against the soft skin there. She trembles in response, and fuck, I'm so damn hard that it hurts.

Her hand goes to my shoulder and I caress her hip and cup her ass. My gaze lifts and her teeth scrape her bottom lip. My teeth go to her hip, where I nip, and then soothe the tiny bite with my tongue. Her lips part and I slide two fingers inside her. She arches her hips and makes a barely there, but fucking sexy as hell, sound. And when I lick her clit, she pants out another little sound that drives me out of my mind.

I rotate her and sit her down on the bed, my hands settling on her knees, my lips finding her inner thigh while my hand works a path up the opposite leg, but I'm done waiting. I slip my shoulders between her legs and my mouth closes down on her sex. When she moans, I pull her forward and force her to her back, lifting her legs to my shoulders, while I start licking and suckling, hungry for more of this woman, and yes, she's right. We're wrong. We're so fucking wrong that we are right in every possible way. That I can sense she isn't one of them is *everything*. Every fucking thing, and I slide two fingers inside her again, reveling in the way she arches her hips, lifting into the thrust of my fingers. I lick her everywhere, the taste of her shifting from salty to sweet when she suddenly quakes into orgasm, her body spasming around my fingers. It's then that I realize I don't have a condom.

I use my fingers and mouth to stroke her to completion, and when she's done, really done, I slide up her body to kiss her, and damn it, the taste of her on both our lips about undoes me. "I don't have a condom," I whisper.

"Oh god," she whispers. "Please tell me no."

"I wish I could," I say kissing her and rolling us to our sides. "No sex."

"I owe you then," she says, her hand on my chest when I want it on my cock. I want it all over my body, but I don't move. I don't touch her. "You owe me nothing."

"I do," she says, "because that was—I um, don't even have words for what that was."

"You don't owe me," I repeat. "I'm not *them*."

She glances down. "Well then," she says, pulling back to look at me. "If I don't owe you, you owe me. I want to taste you coming on my tongue." Her hand slides down my tattoo sleeve. "Because just looking at your ink has me needing more." Suddenly her hand is just where I want it, on my cock, and I'm too busy reveling in how damn good it feels to care when she shoves me to my back and crawls on top of me. Especially since she's naked and gorgeous, and I now have a perfect view of her breasts.

"What are you doing, Harper?" I ask. "We don't have a condom."

She moves to the side of me, her knees at my hip as she runs her hand over my zipper, stroking the hard length of my now throbbing cock. "But we have my mouth." She leans in and kisses my stomach the way I'd kissed hers.

I don't even consider resisting where this is going. Her mouth, my cock. Yes-*fucking-please*. Now. I want her too damn badly to say no and already my hand is on her head, her mouth kissing me through my pants, and there's no real preamble before she has my cock out of my pants and in her hand, but instead of sucking me, she shoves at my pants; as if they're a distraction we can't afford. I'm all about getting rid of the distractions. I sit up, kiss her, and then stand.

I'm fully undressed in thirty seconds, facing her with my cock thick and jutted out, the heat of her eyes on my body, on my erection, driving my urgency. I settle on a knee in front of her, at the same moment she rises to her knees to meet me there. Those beautiful full lips of hers part and lift, and I can't resist another taste. I kiss her, a deep slide of tongue, the taste of her so damn sweet that I want to get lost in her. I take us down to the mattress, side by side and fuck, I know we don't have a condom, but I just want to feel the wet heat of her body pressed against me for a moment.

I press into the V of her body and deepen the kiss, my hands all over her body, her body molded close, both of us desperate in a way I don't ever remember being desperate. I reach between us and stroke my cock along her sex. "Eric," she whispers, her fingers curling on my chest. "We don't have a condom."

"I know that. I just want to feel you for one moment. Just one." I press inside her, sinking deep but I don't let myself move. "Holy fuck," I murmur, and I know I have to stop now but I slide back and thrust once more.

She gasps. "We have to stop," she whispers urgently but then we're kissing, and it's so damn good, too good. I'm going to fucking come if I don't stop now.

I pull out and we both pant with the impact. "Holy hell, woman," I say rolling to my back in pain with just how close I was to coming inside her, all that wet, tight heat enveloping me.

Harper rolls to my side, her soft, perfect curves pressed to my side, and she leans in and kisses me. "I really wish you were still inside me," she whispers against my lips, her voice so damn sweet and sexy, her hand sliding down my chest and over my stomach to grip my cock. "What do you need right now?" she asks.

"To be fucking you," I say. "In about ten different ways our lack of a condom says I can't."

"We can still do this," she says. "I can still do this." She doesn't use words to explain what "this" is. She slides down my body, her hand still wrapped around my shaft, as she settles on her knees beside me. Her eyes meeting mine, her tongue licking away the liquid pooling at the tip of my shaft, which I'm pretty sure is more than simple arousal. I don't even want to think about how close I was to coming inside her. She takes care of that mental rabbit hole though. She closes her mouth around me, sucking me long and deep, her tongue sliding around me as she does, and I tell myself to stop, I tell myself that I was so close to coming inside her, that it won't take much for me to come in her mouth. I try to stop. I try damn hard to pull her back. "Stop, Harper, or I'm going to—"

She sucks me deeper and it's all over. I can't hold back. I thrust into her mouth and I'm done. One more thrust and I'm shuddering with release and I can't pull back. She sucks me deeper, longer, and then slower until she's taken me all the fucking way. God, I think I'm in love with this woman, which of course, isn't possible. I don't do love, but if I did, I'd already be halfway there with all her vulnerable sexiness.

When she releases me and kisses my stomach, I drag her to me, kissing her and rolling her to her back. "I really hate that I don't have a condom."

"I don't," she says. "It means you're not a manwhore who's always prepared to fuck anyone, but I know it's just this. You're leaving. You don't want this. I feel that."

"I want you," I say, shocked at how completely I mean those words.

"I don't mean me. I mean this place."

"Why do *you* want this place?" I ask. "What makes you need this?"

"What made *you* need it?" she counters, avoiding a direct answer.

"Family. I needed the connection."

"And now?"

"No," I say easily, the answer that wasn't clear when I arrived is clear now. "Not now."

"I wish I didn't need this." She rolls off of me and onto her back. "Why do you call me princess?"

I glance over at her. "You're the heir to a business that Kingston absorbed. You're royal blood in these parts, just not the right royal blood."

"I can't accept that. I can't just let my father's work be absorbed and forgotten. My mother—she made a mistake.

My father worked too hard to have everything he created be forgotten with this merger."

I roll over and settle on top of her, my elbow by her head. "It's done. It's too late and Isaac will always be number one. You know that, right?"

"I don't accept that. Not at all. Isaac—he's the bastard. And worthless. He's about him, not about the company, not about the legacy or the future or—anything that matters."

"He's the heir, the first blood, the golden child."

"I want you to be wrong."

I search her eyes and find the truth. "But you know I'm not," I say.

"Then why are you here? If you really believe that, if you believe we can't make a difference, why are you here?"

She hits a nerve and I roll to my back. "I needed to know I wasn't wrong."

"About your father?"

"About me," I say and I can feel her looking at me but I don't look at her.

"What does that mean?" she asks.

"I needed to know that I knew who I was, who I am."

"Which is who?" she presses.

"The bastard." Now I look at her, now I let her see the real me in my eyes. I let her see who she just half fucked. "I'm him. I will always be him."

"I have much I could say about that," she comments, more thoughtfully than anything.

"I'm listening," I say, certain this is going to be the moment she convinces me we're of two different worlds, when right here, in this bed, we feel like we're of one. I want her to convince me. I want her to give me every reason to get the hell out of this place, her included.

"You're different than anyone I've ever met," she says, running her hand down my ink and tracing one of the many rows of numbers on my forearm.

"Meaning what?"

Her eyes shift from my ink to my face. "You're brave. It takes someone brave to be different and embrace it. I like that you're the bastard but not for the reasons you might think."

I'm remarkably on edge waiting for her to continue but she doesn't make me wait long. She seems to know where she's going and gets there quickly. "Because you embrace it. Because you don't do what they expect. Because you do you, and most of us don't even know what that means."

"Meaning you?"

"Definitely me, but maybe I'll get there. I'm trying. I don't know why I just told you that. I shouldn't have told you that."

I reach up and twine strands of her silky hair in my fingers. "Why?"

Her cellphone rings, a muffled sound in the distance that has her eyes going wide. "Oh God," she whispers, jerking away from my hand to sit up. "Oh God. I'm giving a speech. I'm late." She scrambles off the bed and rushes to locate her clothes, dashing for the living room to dress.

I follow her and stand up. By the time I put my pants on and locate her by the door, she's fully dressed. "I have to go," she says, and I'm stunned at how much I don't want her to leave.

I grab her and pull her to me, kissing the hell out of her before I release her and open the door because if I don't let her go now, I won't. But she doesn't go. She seems to forget her speech, frozen in place, right here in the cottage with me. Those gorgeous blue eyes of hers fixed on me, and I want to know what she's thinking, what she wants, because I want her. Time stretches for several more beats before she closes the space between us and kisses me. "I've changed my mind," she confesses. "I really do hate that we didn't have that condom." With that, she rushes out of the door. I let her go, but fuck, I can't walk away. I can't *really* let her go. She's why I'm still here. She's why I'm not leaving. I'm *not* leaving.

I get dressed again, the scent of her, all sweet and feminine, on my skin, drugging me the way she seems to drug me. I need to see her again. I need to be inside that woman, and not just her body. I want to know why she feels insecure, and she does. I want to know why she's here when she could be so many other places, like with me. It's a crazy, out-of-character thought that I shove aside.

Nevertheless, I pursue her, walking down the path and find the party again. The crowd is still thick, the clusters of tuxedos and gowns gathered around a stage at the end of the pool, and there she is, Harper is on the stage. She's standing next to my father and my asshole of a brother, with her look-a-like mother, who's fifteen years my father's junior, standing next to her. She takes the microphone and starts speaking about the business and the family and damn it, my father kisses her cheek and I know I'm wrong about her. She's one of them. She's not a reason to stay. What the hell was I even thinking?

I turn away and walk down the path to the cottage, pack my bag, and with her still on my tongue, I leave.

Forever this time.

CHAPTER FIVE

Eric

I'm sitting at my desk, in my corner office of the Bennett Firm, working on a buy-in on a sports team that's sure to add a few billion in sales on the books for the company and myself. Which is my job. Make money. Grow the business beyond worldwide legal services. Repeat, with Grayson's aggressive, but smart, stance on growth that works for us in ways it might not for other companies. I'm scanning the final contract when Grayson pokes his head in the door. "I have contract questions." He taps his Rolex. "It's seven o'clock. Let's talk somewhere that isn't here."

"Here-here to that," I say. "I could use a Macallan right about now." I stand up and roll my sleeves down before I shrug on my jacket, which never quite covers my tattoo sleeve, but I really don't give a shit. I'm long beyond giving a shit what anyone thinks of me. If they don't like my ink, they can move on and hope to make money elsewhere. Good riddance and good luck.

"Mia doesn't like clause eight," Grayson says, crossing his arms in front of his chest.

Mia being his fiancée and a criminal attorney with the firm, who's recently re-joined our inner circle and I'm damn glad she is back in his life after a year-long breakup. Whereas I'm a loner, a man without ties, Grayson needs Mia. I might not understand that kind of bond, but I understand him. "She's right. I already told the team owners to go fuck themselves over that clause."

23

He chuckles. "Of course you did, and probably not any nicer than you just told me."

"Probably not," I say. "I take it Mia has trial prep tonight?"

"She does," he says. "She's passionate about this woman she's defending. She's all in."

I shove my MacBook and a stack of papers in my briefcase and join him on the other side of the desk. "We're about to hit the holidays. When's the trial?"

"January."

"And the wedding is in March. Are you sure you don't need to push the wedding back?"

"Hell no, we aren't pushing the wedding back. Mia's trying to shut down the prosecution before this even goes to trial. I hired help and we already planned this once. We're just duplicating the past plans."

We head for my door and talk through a few pieces of the contract. We've just stepped into the lobby when the door opens and I'm suddenly standing face to face with a familiar brunette who's the last person I expect to see right now. "What are you doing here, princess?" I ask softly, reminding her of that night we spent together, reminding her that I know who and what she is, then and now.

"Obviously," she says, "I'm looking for you." Her eyes meet mine, blue eyes the color of a perfect sky, and I have no idea why I don't remember this about her. Except I do remember, randomly and too often, just as I'm thinking about all the perfect curves beneath another black dress she's wearing today. This one is more demure, but it doesn't matter. I know what's beneath. I know where my hands and mouth have been and so does she.

As if she's read my thoughts, she cuts her gaze abruptly and focuses on Grayson. "I'm Harper Evans," she says, offering him her hand. "I'm the—"

"I know who you are," Grayson says, shaking her hand, a hand free of a wedding band. "And he told me quite a lot about you," he adds. "I must say that you're as beautiful as he claimed." Grayson does nothing without purpose. He wants her to know I spoke about her to take her off guard, to make her wonder what else I said about her. That's how he works. He discreetly takes control and in this case, he's discreetly handed it to me.

"Thank you," she says, her attention returning to me, the awareness between us downright sizzling, as hot as it had been six years ago. "Can I please speak to you in private?"

Grayson's hand comes down on my shoulder. "Meet me at our usual spot."

I give him a small incline of my head and he departs. "Let's go to my office."

She swallows, her long, graceful neck bobbing with the action, drawing my gaze, and I wonder why I didn't kiss her there when I had the chance. I wonder what the hell it is about this woman, out of all of the women out there, that has stayed with me all these years. That's still with me, right here and now. "This way," I say, motioning her forward, and at this late hour, there's no one in our path, my secretary included.

We walk side by side down the hall, and I'm acutely aware of her by my side, memories of pulling her into the cottage and pressing her against the wall in my mind. We reach my office and I open the door, motioning her forward. She glances at me and I sense that she wants to say something, but she seems to change her mind. She moves forward and I know what she'll see: an executive desk, a window with a view to kill for, and a seating area to the right, which I plan to avoid. I still want her beyond reason and the six years since we last saw each other, and that isn't to my advantage when she clearly wants something from me.

I press my hands on my desk and I say to her what she once said to me. "You want something from me."

She steps to the front of my desk and meets my stare. She's older now, and I see the time both in her blossomed beauty but also in the experience in her eyes, in the jaded history I don't pretend to know firsthand, but I understand in ways few others could. "I do want something from you," she says. "And I wish I could reply to that statement in the way you once did to me, without wanting anything but what was in the moment. Obviously, you didn't. You left."

"I told you I was leaving."

"I know." She doesn't add to that statement but there's more there. "I need help."

Now she has my attention. "What kind of help?"

"I know that you are damn near a billionaire now. Or maybe you are already. I know that you did all this yourself and you have no reason to look beyond here."

"What kind of help?" I repeat.

"We just had our second recall at Kingston Motors and this time after two people died in our cars."

"I read that."

"Something doesn't add up," she says, sounding earnest. "Nothing has changed in our process and on the books and inside our operations, everything looks right, but it's not."

They've grown too fast, I think, but I don't voice that opinion. "What does Isaac say?"

"For me to leave it alone. He has it handled, but our stock is down and I'm not you. I don't have the same head for numbers but I have a decent aptitude. There's money moving in unpredictable ways. I need your help, Eric. Please. It wasn't easy to come here. Not after you left, but I'm here."

After I left.

She keeps saying that like she expected me to stay and while I could find all kinds of pleasure in this woman wishing she'd had more time with me, I'm just too damn jaded myself to see this that simply. She said I wanted something. The reverse could have been true.

"I really need your help," she repeats.

If this was that cut and dry, she'd have my attention, but it's not. There's more to her visit. There's more to this story. I sense it. I see it in her eyes. "What aren't you telling me?" I narrow my eyes on hers and lean forward, my hands on the desk again, pinning her in a stare. "No," I amend. "Let me rephrase. What don't you want me to know?"

CHAPTER SIX

Harper

I knew coming here was trouble but I didn't expect to stare into this man's blue eyes from across the desk and melt all over again. I was certain I'd built the attraction up into more than it was over time, certain I'd turned it into more than it was, but I was wrong. He affects me and not just physically. I mean, yes, he's one hell of a good-looking man and he wears that expensive suit he's got on like he owns it and the world, but it's more with him. There is something raw and dark about him that reaches beyond his sharp cheekbones and jawline. Something in his eyes, something I feel in every part of me, that I hunger to understand. Which of course, I won't, considering why I'm here and who I am.

"What aren't you telling me, Harper?" he demands again.

Too much, I think. So much. I focus on the only part of any of this that might matter to him. "People died, Eric. I'm here to make sure no one else does."

"And whose idea was it for you to come here?"

"I wanted to come after the first recall," I say. "I did. I should have."

His eyes narrow. "Who sent you?"

And there it is. The question I hate with the answer that he'll hate. "Gigi, but—"

"Holy fuck," he growls, pushing off the desk at the mention of his grandmother's name. "You should have left that part out. *No* to anything and everything she wants, now or ever."

I lean on the desk. "Eric."

"Don't look at me with those big blue eyes and say my name and expect anything but another orgasm. And if you came here thinking the fact that I already gave you one influences me, you were wrong. I can want, and do, when it comes to fucking you, and it changes nothing."

My body defies the level head I'm trying to have right now. It remembers that orgasm. It remembers his hands. It wants more, but he's trying to rattle me and I understand why. I know his past. I know why Gigi is the plague to him. I push off the desk. "I don't think an orgasm, or two since you had one as well in case you've forgotten, influences you. I'm just asking that you hear me out."

"For the record," he says. "I remember both orgasms with crystal clarity. I also remember everything about Gigi."

"I know, and I could have lied and told you I made this decision on my own, but I feel like I'm swimming in lies back at Kingston. I don't want them with you, too. I know Gigi was horrible to your mother. She told me that. She has regrets over trying to deny her, and you, your rightful place in the company."

"My place in the company? My mother was sick and we were living in a shithole of a trailer park we could barely afford. I'm pretty sure she didn't give a shit about my place in the company. I damn sure don't." He inhales, seeming to rein himself in before he folds his arms in front of his broad, perfect chest, his tattoo sleeve partially exposed. The tattoos that I know tell a story that I am certain has a lot to do with Gigi and his mother. "That woman doesn't have regrets," he adds. "Saying she does is a lie."

"She was horrible to me, too, but I was with her when she had a small heart attack a year ago. It changed her."

"Nothing changes who we are at the core and if you really believe that, then you're as naive as you were six years ago."

"Naive?" I repeat, my voice low and calm when I really want to punch him right now. "I guess if I was naive, we can blame my decision to get half naked with my stepbrother on me being young and stupid." It's out before I can stop the words that place our intimate past right here in this room.

28

His eyes darken and heat. "Why would we do that? It wasn't a mistake."

"It was a mistake," I assure him, "for about ten different reasons I'm not going to list."

"The mistake was me thinking you weren't one of them," he says dryly.

I feel those words like a punch, with guilt I shove away before he reads it and me. "I'm not one of them," I say and I don't have to cut my gaze as I'm certain he expects. I've never meant those words like I do now. "I told you why I'm with them. This is a piece of my father."

"Six years is a long time to work with someone you're not devoted to," he muses. "And you're trusted enough to be their spokesperson to me."

"They don't know I'm here," I say, trying not to think of the hell that will follow if they find out or the many things about this past six years that he can never know.

"Gigi is them," he says. "If she knows, they know."

"She's been shut out."

"She's the primary stockholder."

"Who isn't exactly in great health. Your father threatened to go to the board to get her removed as CEO."

He rounds the desk and we turn to face each other and damn it, he smells just as earthy and perfect as I remember. And he's so big and overwhelmingly male. He's also had his tongue in all kinds of places and I need to not go there. He arches a brow. "What are you thinking, Harper?"

"A lot of things," I say, and avoiding the past we share, I hold out my hands. "You've done so much. You're brilliant. They all know that. We need you."

"We or Gigi?"

"*We* need you, but Gigi said to tell you she's begging. This is her life's work. She's terrified of losing it."

His brutal perfect mouth quirks. "I'd almost be willing to go there just to watch her beg like my mother did for help."

His mother who killed herself. What was I thinking coming here? "This was a mistake. I should have just told her we'd find another way." I try to turn away but he catches my elbow, heat radiating up my arm. My gaze rockets to his and that connection I'd felt to him six years ago is present and accounted for, thickening the air between us.

"If there's another way," he says, "why come to me?"

"People died, and you're a genius, *literally*. You also have an understanding of the company, a connection, your family."

"Family? Like being the stepbrother who gave you an orgasm?"

"Now you're just being an asshole and you have a right. I get that, too, but I didn't do any of the things they did to you. Like I said. This was a mistake. Forget I was here." I jerk away from him and rush for the door, feeling as if my heart is going to explode in my chest on the way. I reach for the knob, escape only seconds away.

Eric is suddenly behind me, his hand on the door, his big body crowding mine, so close that I can almost feel his body heat. "Tell me why you're really here."

I rotate to face him and that's a mistake. He's overwhelmingly right here, in front of me. "Just let me leave."

He studies me for several intense beats, those blue eyes so damn probing and intelligent. "You had to know that I wasn't going to help."

"I know that, but I had to try. *People have died.*"

"You came here because people have died."

"I keep saying that."

"But it's not everything. It's not the whole reason."

"It's the reason I was willing to come here and I know you might not believe me, but considering our past, this wasn't easy for me."

"Because I left or because you regret what happened between us?"

"Does it matter? I was one of them to you then and I'm one of them now."

He considers me for a long few beats. "I know that you have a trust fund from your father. Take it and run. Get the hell out now because you're right, even watching from a distance, and I am, there's a problem at Kingston."

I have a fleeting moment of fear that he knows because he's somehow involved, but I shove that idea away. He's not behind this. I know too much about what really is happening to believe he's behind this. "What do you know that I don't know?"

"To get out. I got out. You need to as well."

"I don't get my trust fund until I turn thirty-five and my mother loaned it to your father."

"You're fucking kidding me."

"No. No, I'm not."

"Then leave them and come here. I'll give you a job. You can make your way just like I did. Unless you don't trust your ability to make your own way?"

"I was planning to leave. I told your grandmother right before her heart attack."

"And that made you feel guilty?"

"What part of *people have died* do you not understand? I can't just walk away and your grandmother really has changed. She's old. She can't handle this alone."

He doesn't immediately reply. He just stands there, looking at me, seconds ticking by before his gaze sweeps my mouth, his body so close to my body, and Lord help me, I think he might kiss me. I think I want him to kiss me, but he doesn't. He pushes off the door. "The job offer stands. Safe travels, Harper, because we both know you won't stay."

My lashes lower with the rejection I've felt not once now but twice with this man. I open my eyes and force my gaze to his. "Thank you for seeing me." I open the door and exit, my knees weak as I rush through the offices and toward the elevator. I punch the button and the doors open, allowing me to rush inside, but once I'm there, alone in the car, reality hits hard.

I *am* alone. Eric isn't going to help me.

CHAPTER SEVEN

Eric

I stand there in my office, staring at the doorway, hot and hard, with the scent of Harper's perfume in the air, the memories of her naked and in my arms in my mind. I want her. I have always wanted her, but we aren't even close to possible. She's on top of the Kingston throne. I will never kneel to that throne, and yet, she has stayed with me all these years. Maybe because *she's* on that throne. Maybe because she's untouchable. Maybe because she has those damn beautiful eyes. All I really know is that me wanting her this fucking bad makes her a weakness that every Kingston, perhaps her included, would happily use against me.

I want to believe her intentions are pure, but six years in the folds of that family make that damn hard. I'd also like to believe that I know more about what's happening at Kingston than her, which would make her visit authentic. I scrub my jaw and cross to my desk, where I grab my briefcase and head for the door. I have a deal to close and money to make for a man who deserves his success.

By the time I'm in a hired car on the way to the bar in Grayson's apartment building, I've replayed every word of that conversation with Harper ten times, but I keep going back to Gigi, that bitch of a woman who all but ensured my mother's miserable death. I hate her at least ten degrees deeper than I do my father, who at least saved his punishment for me, not my mother. The car drops me at my destination and I walk inside to find Grayson in his normal booth.

33

He lifts the bottle he's ordered, an expensive-ass whiskey I welcome right about now. "I thought you might need this."

"In duplicate," I say, settling into the booth as he fills my glass.

I down the contents and pull a contract from my briefcase to get to work. "Where were we?"

He arches a brow. "Where were we? Talking about Harper."

"There's nothing to talk about."

"You damn near turned down this job to go back there again and we both know it was over her."

"That was when I thought she was too green to protect herself." I refill my glass. "She's been with them for six years. She doesn't need her hand held."

"She knows the company's in trouble," he assumes, downing his own drink.

"She knows."

"And?" he prods when I offer nothing more.

"You aren't going to let this go, are you?"

"No," he says. "Because friends don't let friends deal with shit alone, as you've proven over and over both professionally and personally. Talk to me."

"We have a contract to deal with."

"That we'll handle."

I inhale and let out a breath. "She wants me to go to Denver. She wants me to save them."

"Them or her?"

"Both. My grandmother sent her."

"Gigi?" he asks, incredulously. "Why would she think that you would ever help Gigi?"

"Obviously, that's why Gigi sent Harper. Or the whole clan of them sent her."

"You think they know you two hooked up?" he asks.

"When I look into her eyes, no, I don't believe she'd tell them or use me. When I'm with that woman, I'm one hundred percent into her. She seems honest, sweet, smart, too smart to be with those assholes. When I step back like now, I see six years of her with them. Something doesn't add up."

"You almost went back to them ju;
family unit," he reminds me. "Maybe she .

"It doesn't feel right."

"But she does, correct? She's not one ol

His question comes from understandi.
person I talk to, the only person in this wc
outside of a few of my SEAL buddies, and ゜ ᴗak.
We'd die for each other, and be there for eacl ᴗ∪er with one
phone call, but they don't know me beyond blood and
sacrifice. Grayson does. He knows about the moment I saw
her on that stage. He knows how it affected me. He knows
how I reasoned that away, as some Bastard/Princess head
game I'd put on myself. "Six years, Grayson," I repeat. "That's
loyalty, not obligation."

"But she doesn't feel like one of them," he presses. "You
keep saying that for a reason, and you have the best instincts
I've ever seen."

"I have a head for numbers. I have a head for statistics.
That's not this. I can't trust my instincts when it comes to a
woman I want to fuck. Maybe I just want what I didn't have
or can't have."

He studies me for several long moments, not entertaining
my musings. He gets right to the point. "You don't want to
turn your back on her. What are you going to do?"

"I told her to get out of there and I offered her a job."

"Which you knew she'd decline," he comments, lifting his
glass in my direction. "Where does that leave you and her?"

"I made sure she knows the door is open. She can leave."

"You mean she can come to you." He leans forward. "Do
you really think she knows she can come to you?"

"I repeated the offer more than once."

"In a short meeting after a six-year wait for a reunion.
How do you know anything about her and her motives at this
point?" He taps the table. "Let's be honest. Let's get to the
meat of this. We both know the state of that company for
reasons you probably don't want to share with Harper. We
both know there are things going on that spell trouble."

"Get to the meat, Grayson."

How much trouble is that for her? Is she in danger? Maybe she can't get out without your help. Maybe she was afraid to tell you that, for reasons we can both surmise. You could turn on her."

"*Fuck.* Stop already."

"Do you care what happens to her?"

"I barely know her."

"And yet you never forgot her. That's how this works. It's how it worked for me with Mia. I met her and it was her. It was never going to be anyone else."

It's not her, I think. It won't ever be her. He just doesn't get the dynamic between me and this woman. He can't. He's never been the bastard. He's a better version of Isaac, the heir, and Grayson is the king now that his father is gone. I tap the contract. "Work. Money. *Your* money. *Now.*"

His lips quirk. "I hit about ten nerves, I see."

"Clause eight," I say, and once I start talking, I distract him with business, even if my mind is constantly going to Harper. Is she in danger? *I need help.* She said that several times.

I'm still thinking about those words when Mia appears by the table, looking gorgeous in a pink dress, her long dark hair loose around her shoulders. "Hello, you two handsome men." She slides into the booth and kisses Grayson, her hand settling on his jaw. "I missed you."

I have no idea what it is about this moment that gets to me. I see these two together all the damn time and I never think of me with someone else, but right now, I'm thinking about Harper. I'm thinking about me with Harper. "Fuck," I murmur, pushing out of the booth and grabbing my phone from my pocket.

I step outside, welcoming the cold October night, and I dial Blake Walker of Walker Security, a man who's not only a world class hacker and ex-ATF agent, he and his team, just helped us through another nightmare. I trust them. "Eric," he greets. "What's up?"

"Kingston Motors."

"I know the connection to you," he offers without prodding. "I make it a point of knowing the people I'm working with."

"Good. This will go faster then. Find out what's dirty there. If you can't get real answers, hack the financials with enough detail to allow me to dissect it all. Look at the officers, especially my half-brother and father."

"What else?"

"I'll email you a list of questions on my mind in a few minutes. I need this to be comprehensive. Take the time you need. What I need now: find out if my grandmother had a heart attack about a year ago. Text me the information."

"I can tell you that now." I can hear him banging on his keyboard and I wait, every nerve in my body on edge and I know why. I need one little piece of information proven to be honest, a pebble of truth that might indicate she isn't lying to me.

"Yes," Blake finally says. "She did, in fact, have a heart attack, but she's now recovered."

"Harper Evans," I say, relieved with his response but already wanting more. "I need to know everything there is to know about her and tonight."

"I can get you an overview tonight. The rest will have to be tomorrow."

"That works." I hang up and Grayson steps outside with me.

"You need to go deal with this."

"I need to be here closing this deal," I argue.

"You are more than capable of doing both. Close it from the road. She got to you, then and now, and this is your blood family."

"If I go there, I won't save them. I'll finish them off."

"Then maybe you need to go to her tonight and convince her to take the job. Or not. I just know that you don't have closure. I feel it. I see it. You need it. Go get it, and her, like you get everything else you decide you want." He doesn't wait for an answer. He walks back inside the bar.

I don't stand there and think about his words. He knows me and he's right. I need closure, not with my family, but with Harper. I pull my phone back out and dial Blake. "Give me an hour, man," he says when he answers. "I'm good, but I still require time."

"Harper's in town tonight. I need to know which hotel."

CHAPTER EIGHT

Harper

After contemplating tucking tail and licking my wounds on an early return flight home, I decide against that cowardly action. I'm going to talk to Eric again tomorrow. Tonight, I'll wallow in room service and champagne, when I usually don't drink. Of course, champagne is the drink of celebration and I'm far from celebrating, but it's my favorite drink, so I'm improvising and turning it into a pity party drink.

Pity works well for me.

I'll wallow and then get it out of my system and fight again.

And it's a hell of a pity party, considering I've been dumped by the hottest man I've ever known not once, but twice. He's too good at goodbye. I'm too good at wanting him. I have let one night with that man affect me in lingering ways that make no sense.

I sit down on the love seat in the corner of the room and fill my glass, since I ordered a champagne dinner before I decided that was a bad idea, and right after pulling on sweats and a tee; because I'm feeling really, really sexy tonight after Eric barely gave me a blink. Once my bubbly is in my glass and I'm sipping, I think about how Eric affects me. That man makes me feel everything, and I don't even know what that means. I'm just aware in every physical and emotional way when he's in the room and no one else has done that to me. I've tried to make it happen. I've dated. I've dated attractive, powerful, sexy men who did absolutely nothing for me. It's ridiculous. I was with Eric one night and we didn't even have real sex.

The doorbell rings, and yes, there's a doorbell because that's just how they roll around here, I guess. I down my champagne and stand up, the buzz of two glasses hitting me rather suddenly. Clearly, I should have waited for my food before I indulged in the champagne. After all, what have I eaten today? Not much. Some cashews, I think. Does Starbucks count as a meal?

I cross the room and open the door, only to suck in a stunned breath to find Eric standing there, his jacket and tie gone, his brightly colored ink that was once up and down one arm now on both. I stare at that ink, intrigued by the random designs—a timepiece, a skull, numbers—lots of numbers and the heat of his stare has me snapping my gaze back to his face, those blue eyes fixing me in a piercing stare.

I can't breathe. Why do I react like this to this man? "I thought you were room service."

Those gorgeous lips of his quirk. "I can be."

"Don't say things like that."

I don't even have time to process him moving, and he's right here in front of me, his hands on my waist, sending a rush of heat all over my body as he walks me inside the room. The door slams behind him, and suddenly we're so very alone. "Why wouldn't I say things like that, princess? We have unfinished business. I know you feel it, too."

My hand flattens on his chest and his heart thunders beneath my palms, and that tells a story. He's not as cold as I'd felt he was when I left his office. He's just as present as I am in this reunion, just as affected by us being together again, but I don't fool myself into thinking this means more than it should. I'm certain this need between us comes from another place for him than it does me. From anger and conquest of the enemy he believes me to be and I don't want this like that. I twist away from him and quickly place the coffee table between me and him.

"How did you find me?" I demand.

"I'm resourceful," he says, his voice pure silk. "If I wasn't, you wouldn't want me, now would you?" He glances at my champagne. "Celebrating?"

"Wallowing in failure," I say because it's true and I prefer every truth I can embrace, plus I'm buzzing. "And I can't seem to drink anything else."

"I could help you expand your tastes."

There is innuendo in those words that has me snapping back at him. "But you won't be around to expand my tastes, now will you?"

"That depends on you."

"What does that mean? Because if sleeping with you is a negotiation strategy, I don't want to sleep with you."

He closes the space between him and the table and I have nowhere to go. He's in front of me, so close I can smell that earthy scent of him again. He picks up the bottle, reads the label and fills my glass before drinking, his mouth now where my mouth was only minutes before. His eyes twinkle with mischief and suggestion as he says, "It's good," and then adds, "for champagne." He sets the glass down. "And yes, I want to fuck you. No, it's not a negotiation. Fucking you and getting fucked by the Kingston family are not synonymous, even if that's your intent."

"I didn't come here to fuck you, Eric," I snap. "I came for help. Just leave, okay? I told you, forget I was here."

"I can't do that."

"Not until you finish what you started?" I challenge.

"We aren't done with each other. I think we both know that."

"We've been done for six years."

"If we were done, I wouldn't be here right now. You're the only reason I'm here."

I cut my gaze, and I'm back in that night I met him, standing on that stage, staring out at the audience and looking for him. "Harper," he says softly, and when his voice was hard moments before, it's not now.

I force my gaze to his. "I went back to the cottage, hoping you hadn't really left."

His lashes lower and now he cuts his gaze, like the idea of me going there actually affects him, and when he looks at me, his blue eyes are laden with emotions I can't read. "I had to leave."

"I know," I say, because I do. He hates that place. He hates me as an extension. How can I want a man that hates me?

The doorbell rings again and it's sweet relief and my escape. "That's my food. You can go. I know you won't help. I knew almost the moment I walked into the lobby today."

He studies me a moment and turns to the door. My heart squeezes with how easily he's going to leave, how certain his steps, when I just told myself and him that I wanted him to leave. He opens the door and I hurry around the table to greet the delivery person. Eric steps back and allows the woman to enter, and I expect him to exit, but he doesn't. "Where would you like it?" the woman asks of the tray in her hand.

She asks this question of Eric and he arches a brow at me. "Right here," I say, indicating the coffee table.

The woman sets everything up for me and still, Eric doesn't move. I give him a "you can go" look and he returns it with a short shake of his head, a silent no, and the look in his eyes is pure heat. I cut my gaze and sign the ticket with a generous tip. The woman hurries to the door and then I'm alone with Eric again. He saunters to the couch and sits down in front of my tray, and when he tries to lift it, I have no idea why, but it sets me off.

I rush forward, sit next to him and hold down the lid. "You don't get to know what I order or what I like. You left. You're going to leave again. Who I am and what I like is *not* your business." I stand up. "Leave now."

He pushes to his towering height and faces me, and I'm immediately aware that joining him on this side of the table was a mistake. He's close, big, and he smells all earthy and perfect. I have about ten seconds to have that thought before he drags me to him, and my God, he feels just as good as he did back then, and it's too much but not enough. "You keep talking about me leaving," he says. "Why? Because you can't believe that the bastard could walk away from the princess?"

Anger flares hard and fast. "I'm going to forgive you for saying that because I know how they treated you. I know where it comes from, but you told me not to make us about them, but you did, then and now."

"I was wrong when I said it wasn't about them. I saw you up on that stage, with them, a part of them."

"Really? Because I looked for you and saw you leaving."

"I was there just long enough to see who you are."

"You didn't see me at all. You saw what you wanted to see and for a really smart person, that was a shallow way of thinking. You barely knew me. I barely knew you."

"Do you *want* to know me, Harper?"

"It doesn't matter," I say. "You're leaving again. You won't help. You won't—"

"*Do you want to know me*, Harper?"

"I'm pretty sure you've already shown me the parts I need to see and they don't work for me."

"I was pissed when I saw you up there."

"I was pissed when you were gone."

His hand goes to my jaw and he tilts my face to his. "And yet here we are," he says, his mouth lowering, lips just above mine, his warm breath teasing me with the promise of a kiss that I shouldn't want. He's the bastard by his own admission and we both know he revels in living up to that title. He's trouble, but my God, I have long hungered for another taste of that trouble.

CHAPTER NINE

Harper

Eric's mouth closes down on mine and it's like I'm six years in the past. I'm aware of the divide between us and try to resist, but I can't. The taste of him is like a drug on my tongue, addictive, sweet, and impossible not to crave. I know this whole "princess" label is all about conquest and division—his conquest, our division. I tell myself this isn't good. I *know* it's not good. I don't want to be with a man who ultimately hates me and that thought is a dash of cold water on the heat burning between me and this man.

I shove on his chest. "Stop."

"Are we doing this again?" he asks, his voice husky, rough. "Because I really don't think either of us wanted to stop then or now."

"How many times did you stand on a stage or just by their side, Eric? How many times in the years you were part of that family?"

"*That* family?" he challenges. "You mean *your* family?"

"We both inherited them. I didn't ask for them, but you judged me for standing on that stage when we both know you did it, too."

"I'm not on that stage with them anymore."

"You were. For years, you were. We both know you were."

"And you still are."

"No," I say. "I'm not. Me being here isn't about them. I swear to you, Eric. It's not."

His fingers slide back under my hair at my neck and he drags my mouth to his. "Tell me later." I barely have time to inhale the warm breath on my lips and he's kissing me again, a long stroke of his tongue against mine undoes me, weakens my knees, makes every part of me tingle and ache.

"I need to tell you now," I whisper when his teeth scrape my lip. "I need you to hear me."

"Later," he repeats softly, stroking the dampness from my lips. "I'll listen."

"You will?" I pull back to look at him. "Promise me you will because—"

"I will," he says, his mouth closing down on mine and it's pure heat and fire. *He's* pure heat and fire and I feel the shift in us, the need that pushes us past family and divide. There is no divide right here, right now. There is just me and him and a night that was never finished but needs completion. Every part of me is alive in a way it hasn't been since I was last with this man. We are wild, hands touching and tongues tangling, but then suddenly there's a shift between us again and his hand settles between my shoulder blades, molding my chest to his chest.

His lips part from mine and our foreheads come together, both of us breathing heavily, the past between us again, so many questions and unspoken words between us with it, but neither of us wants those things to matter. That feeling is here with us, too. The silent understanding that *later* is, in fact, better. That word complicates our already complicated connection, but there is nothing complicated about the fire between us now or the sense of understanding. We're alike and yet we're different. Both pulled into a world we didn't ask to join, a world that is why we're here now.

"Eric," I whisper, and not because I want to break the silence. Because I have this sense he's waiting on me, needing something I don't understand.

His answer is instant, not in words, but actions. His mouth closes down on mine, and I feel the snap of tension in him; whatever hesitation was in him moments before is gone, and I welcome the deep thrust of his tongue, the press of his hand under my shirt, his touch caressing over my ribcage. My breasts are heavy, heat pooling low in my belly with anticipation of what comes next, and then his hand is on my naked breasts, fingers plucking my nipple.

He pulls back to look at me, the deep blue of his stare flecked with amber heat scorching me inside and out. He drags my tee over my head, tosses it away, and then that smoldering stare of his is raking over my breasts, devouring me in ways that inexplicably no other man ever has. Just him. My sex clenches and when I grab his sleeve, tugging him toward me, he doesn't make me wait.

His gaze collides with mine, and the punch of awareness and attraction between us steals my breath even as his hand returns to my neck as he drags my mouth to his. "God, woman," he says, his voice low, rough, almost guttural, "what the hell are you doing to me?" And this time when he kisses me, I sense the barely caged control, the edge of hunger clawing at him, and me with him.

I reach for the buttons of his shirt and he responds by backing me up until I'm against some wall. I don't even know what wall, and then he releases me just long enough to pull his shirt over his head and toss it. I don't play shy. I've waited too long for this to hold back. My hands go to his hard, really perfect chest, my fingers twining in the light brown hair there. Hair I happen to know forms a line of hair that trails beneath his waistband. I want to lick my way down that path, but there is so much with this man to explore, to experience, even as I contemplate that journey, I'm distracted by his tattoos and my hands move to his new ink, the right shoulder that is now a giant jaguar.

"I love your ink," I dare.

Shadows flicker in his eyes, an edge to his mood now that isn't about sex, but that talk we haven't had. "Do you now?"

"Yes," I say, looking him in the eyes. "Why is that a problem? What just happened? Because I do love it. Very much, and I want to—"

I never finish that sentence, I never get to tell him how much I want my mouth on his ink and his body before his cheek is pressed to mine, his lips at my ear, breath warm on my neck as he declares, "I want you naked" his teeth scrape my earlobe, "in every way, Harper."

My lips part on those words that I don't fully understand and once again, just like six years before, he turns me to the wall and forces me to catch it with my hands. It's a power thing, I know, and it should perhaps bother me. He wants to control me, he *needs* control. It's about him ruling over the royalty, and to him, I'm that royalty and there's nothing I can do about it. He feels like I'm the girl on the throne who's fucking beneath herself.

He yanks my pants down and in seconds they're over my bare feet and I'm completely naked. His hands are all over me, and when he leans in, his lips at my ear, his hands on my breasts, my breath hitches in my throat. "You're mine now, princess. All mine. You get that, right? There's no turning back now."

"I don't want to turn back."

"But will you regret this and me?"

"I regret you leaving. That was a bastard move."

I feel him stiffen, and I don't care. It *was* a bastard move. "Is that right?" He pinches my nipples as if punishing me for the truth, and I try to move my hands, but I'm trapped between that wall and his big body, the thick ridge of his erection at my backside.

He folds himself around me, one hand on my hip, the other on my breast. "You have me now, but you might regret it, because this *bastard* is going to own you before tonight is over, Harper."

CHAPTER TEN

Harper

This bastard is going to own you before tonight is over,
Harper.

Those words, Eric's words, are in the air between us, the
implications of me against the wall and him at my back
leaving no room to question his intent. He wants control. He
has control. His hands go to my shoulders. "How do you feel
about being owned?" he demands, and it's clear we're talking
about a whole lot more than us, naked, tonight.

"They don't own me," I say. "They've never owned me."

"You seem pretty damn owned to me, princess," he says,
squeezing my backside and then giving it a hard smack. I
yelp at the unexpected sting that he squeezes away even as he
steps to my side, caging my legs and cupping my sex. "But
right now, you're mine."

"Because it turns you on to be the bastard that owns me?"
I challenge, hating the way my hands are stuck to this wall,
wanting to touch him, wanting to hit him and kiss him and
ten more things I haven't even considered yet.

"I do believe it does," he says. "Does it turn you on?" He
slides fingers against the wet, slick heat of my body. "I do
believe it does." His lips go to my ear. "Don't worry. I'll make
it hurt really good. But don't worry, I'll only punish you if you
ignore my orders."

"Punish me?" I demand. "What does that even mean?"
His finger slides inside me and I bite back a moan as he pulls
back that finger.

"I can give," he says, "and I can take away."

49

My gaze meets his. "Two can play at that game, you do know that, right?"

He laughs, this low, sexy laugh that I feel in the clenching of my sex and the empty ache he's created there. "We'll see." He rotates to stand behind me again. "Don't move," he orders, "or the next time I put my tongue on you, I won't finish you." With that threat, he steps away from me and I can feel the heat of his stare on my naked body, and the ache between my thighs has me clenching them together. There's a shuffle of clothing and the tear of the condom wrapper, and that's it. I can't take it. I'm all for playing a sexy game with this man, but his reasons for all of this get to me. They really do.

I turn around and my mouth goes dry as I find him naked, rippling, long, lean muscle from head to toe, his cock jutted forward, and the condom is in place. He drags me to him, his erection pressing to my hip. "I told you not to move."

"I've already had your mouth," I say, not even sure where this daring in me is coming from, but it's alive and well with this man.

His eyes spark with amber flecks but there is something more in his gaze, a knife of emotion that I feel like a cut. "Is that right?" he asks, his voice low, raspy.

"Yes," I say, and I feel myself shifting with that shift in him, with that emotion he's bottling up, with something unspoken that I may never understand. Now my voice softens and I react not to the vulnerability I feel with this man, but what I feel, what I need and what I think he needs: every word of truth I can speak. "I hate that you left that night. I'm glad you're here now."

His lashes lower and I have this sense that he doesn't want me to read some emotion in his eyes before he looks at me again and says, "Me too, princess. Me too."

Those words, a few small words, hold so much implication and they expand between us, stealing my breath. We stare at each other and what passes between us is almost too much, it confuses me. It calls to me. He calls to me and I want to know him. I want to understand him. In some ways, I already do and I believe he knows this. Which is exactly why my hand settles on top of the stunningly created jaguar on his arm, and I don't miss the very Kingston-like blue eyes, or the fact that his animal is a symbol of the competing car brand. "Is it a fuck you to Kingston Motors?"

"I'm pretty sure my father considers me a fuck you to the Kingston name." He leans in to kiss me, his mouth lingering just above mine. "I'd have already fucked them if Grayson hadn't held me back. You need to know that."

"I know you don't believe me, but that you could, and you haven't—I like that about you."

He doesn't reply, but seconds tick by before his mouth is on my mouth, and this time, there's no holding back. He's not about control this time. He's about consuming me. He's about drinking me in and touching me and I don't hold back. I have wanted him for so very long. I've compared everyone to him for no justifiable reason except he was a fantasy bigger than life. A man with a common bond and more of an understanding of who and what I am than he ever knew. We are both wild, burning alive, touching each other, but suddenly, he pulls back, staring down at me, searching my face for something, I don't know what.

My fingers find his face, the rasp of stubble on my skin as I trace the strong line of his jaw. His hand covers mine and suddenly he kisses me again, a hard, punishing kiss, as if he's angry. I taste it. I feel it as he smacks my backside again. I yelp and I have no idea why I'm so incredibly aroused by him doing this, but everything with this man is well, everything. And that's it. That's why I'm so damn aroused. This is him. He's more exposed than not. His anger—and he *is* angry—is a piece of him.

"You want to punish me for who I am," I accuse, my fingers curling on his chest. "You want to own me because of who I am."

"I want a lot of things where you're concerned, Harper," he says, tangling rough fingers in my hair. "Too many fucking things."

"The bastard doesn't get to fuck me. Whatever you do, you own. Whatever I do, it's with you, Eric."

"Is that right?"

"Yes. That's right."

His jaw sets hard, his eyes burning a mix of hot fire and anger, I think. He turns me to the bed and before I know his intent, I'm on my knees in front of him. It's then that I realize just how deep his need to own me is. It's not about sex. It's about who I am and who he is. It really is about him owning me and them with me. It's about this moment. It's about now. No matter what I do, I can't change this need in him. I'm not sure I want to change it. Let him own me. In some ways, he has for six long years. I want freedom. I want to know where this leads. I want to know that this man is more than an empty space I can never fill. I want him to occupy it, and me, or set me free.

CHAPTER ELEVEN

Harper

I might not like where Eric's head is right now, but I know until he owns me, until he feels like he has real control, we'll never have a real conversation. I'll never know where this is going. I'll never know why I can't move on from a night six years ago. And I need to know. I need a lot of things right now with this man.

His fingers slide into my sex and sensations rock my body. I arch into the touch, and his cock slides along the seam of my body, back and forth, back and forth, until—oh God—he's pressing inside me. He's stretching me, filling me in a long, slow slide until he's buried deep. And then he pulls back and thrusts hard.

I gasp and his hands shackle my hips, he's driving into me, pumping hard and fast, and I want more, so much more, that I forget what that even means—just more of this man, of this night, of everything where he's concerned. Yes, everything. I forget everything but the pleasure of him inside me until suddenly he stops and leans into me, his face buried against my back, his cock still throbbing inside me. "Eric," I breathe out, confused, and aching for more.

He shifts and pulls out of me, and before I can recover the shock to my body, we're on the bed, and he's pulling me to face him, lifting my leg and pressing back inside me; filling me again, and when he's buried deep once more, he strokes my hair from my face and tilts my gaze to his. "I decided I wanted you to know who's fucking you."

"Because you want me to know the bastard son fucked me?"

"No, Harper. Because I want you to know, that I, Eric, came here for *you*, not them. Just you."

My hand goes to his face. "I didn't come for them. I swear to you, this isn't for them. It's for me and my father's legacy. I need your help and—"

He brushes his lips over mine. "Just be here with me right now. This is just us. I'm leaving them out of it. I wasn't, but I am now. You leave them out of it, too." He strokes the dampness from my lips. "Just me and you and years of regret, because I *do* regret leaving."

"You do?"

"You, not them." His lips curve. "I should have gotten a box of condoms and then taken you someplace far away and used every damn one of them."

I laugh and smile, too. "Yes. Yes, you should have."

His mouth comes down on mine, and the energy shift between us is sharp and yet rich with passion and emotion. It's gentler. It's deeper. The press of tongue to tongue a caress, not a demand. The soft sway of his body against mine, seductive and slow. His kisses drink me in, seem to savor the taste of me as I do him, but at some point, I don't know when we snap. His hand cups my backside and he pulls me hard against him, his fingers stroking my sex from behind even as he pumps into me. We need now. We need so much and yet the feeling is there—the sense that we can't have more, yet we have to have it. We have to have each other. I have never felt anything like it. I have never wanted anything like this. I have never kissed anyone like I would die without the next lick of his tongue, but I do Eric.

We sway and grind and pump until that rise to pleasure is to the level of no return. I can't stop the tumble into release and my sex clenches around him, his low, guttural groan my reward, the shudder of his body following. We ride the rush of release together and when we collapse, we hold onto each other, but as seconds tick by, reality seeps into the room, and I can almost feel it trying to pull us apart. He hates the Kingstons and he won't help me. I know what's coming. We both know what's coming and that's another goodbye, but it won't come with any more closure than we had six years ago.

At least not for me.

He's right. He owned me tonight. In some ways, he's owned me for six years. I fear that he still will when I leave this city, no doubt now without him, but deep down, I know that's for the best. There are things back in Denver that divide us. Things I forgot by coming here. If he goes back there, he will ruin them, or they'll own him. That means this was never going to work. He strokes my hair, a gentle, regretful touch like he's thinking the same thing as me, but he doesn't speak.

He pulls out of me before rolling away and sitting up to toss the condom in a trashcan. I suddenly feel naked and exposed but it doesn't matter what I feel. It doesn't matter how much I don't want to push him. No thought I just had about this being a bad idea matters. There are reasons it can't matter. I have to push him. I start to roll away to get dressed and ready for battle, but he's already back, catching my arm and now we're both naked on our knees on the bed, facing each other.

"Running away?" he challenges.

"No. Not at all. I need your help. I know how much you hate them. I know they deserve it, but I'm desperate and I didn't sleep with you for help. I know it might seem that way, so you know, fucking the princess bitch seems just fine to you, but it's not that to me."

"That's not what this was to me," he says.

"It was. It was at first and you know it."

"No. It's me not wanting to get fucked by you as an extension of them."

"I'm not them, but I need help with them."

"I won't help them."

"Help *me*."

"I will. Come here. I'll give you a job at double the pay you make there and there are no conditions. If we never fuck again, we don't fuck again. I can place you in any state, or several countries, for that matter. I'll get you a new start."

"My mother—"

"Take her with you."

"She won't leave him," I say. "She married my father young. They were in love. Losing him left her devastated. Your father took over her life and her money when she was vulnerable and not in a good way. I can't leave her. Not in the way you suggest."

"You said you were going to leave."

"Before the recalls," I remind him. "Before she could end up in trouble with the rest of them. I *have* to go back. Go back with me."

"If I go back there, I'll finish them off. I won't save them. Still want me to go with you?"

"Yes. I do. Because I don't believe you're the bastard you want everyone to believe you are or you would have already done it."

"You're wrong." His jaw sets. "And there's nothing more to say, at least not by me." In other words, there's more to say, and I'm the one who has to say it. And there is, but I'm not sure any of it changes anything. It might even make it worse.

He releases me, leaving me cold and aching for his touch. I want this man. Some part of me needs him beyond logic. Maybe it's the connection to something we both want to be home that never really can be home. Maybe it's more. I really don't know or want to understand. It doesn't matter. He's no longer touching me and maybe he never will again.

He's already dressing and somehow that feels like a slap. Me naked on the bed while he dresses certainly feels cold and done. He's done. He's made his decision to leave, probably before he ever arrived. He wanted to fuck me. He wanted to own me. It was all part of what he's just declared. He wants to ruin his father and brother. I'm nothing more than an extension of them. God, I'm a fool but what did I expect? The minute I got naked with him, it must have seemed like I was fucking him to get a favor.

Embarrassed, I scramble off the bed and find my sweats, pulling them on. Once we're both dressed, he walks to my room service tray and opens it. "Macaroni and cheese," he says.

"My favorite food," I reply and I have no idea why this feels almost as intimate of an admission as anything else between us tonight. I regret sharing this part of me with him, but then, why wouldn't I? I'm just a revenge fuck to him.

He walks to me and I tell myself to back away. I tell myself to end this now, but I can't stand the idea of never touching him again. I can't resist the need to feel his hands on my body just one more time. I suck in air, waiting for it, wanting it, and when he slides his hand under my hair to my neck, I feel this man, who would be my enemy by his own definition, everywhere, inside and out.

"Just one of the many things," he says, "that I would have liked to have known about you, Harper." He kisses me, a light brush of lips over lips, and then he pulls back. "But that can't happen. There's something you haven't told me. You haven't been honest with me and that makes you one of them." He releases me and walks to the door.

I want to scream at him that I'm not one of them, but I don't, I can't. Because in ways I don't want to be, I am. I have to let him walk out the door and he does. He's gone. I'm alone, but no matter how I connect to his family, I'm still a fish in a sea of Kingston sharks, and I'm going to have to grow my own teeth.

CHAPTER TWELVE

Harper

In life, there are people who really are like two ships passing in the sea never meant to stop or know one another, but what happens when they do?

The idea of leaving New York City and Eric behind is brutal, as if I'm leaving a piece of myself, and that's just nuts. Last night was sex, nothing more. Six years ago was also sex, nothing more. He came. He made me come. He left. He didn't look back. And yet here I am, fretting over leaving without seeing him again, to the point that I'm pacing my hotel room and contemplating skipping my flight with a deep need to see Eric again clawing at me.

I tell myself it's because I need his help, but I know this runs deeper for me. That man affects me and if I wanted closure that allowed me to move on from that party six years ago, and him, I didn't get it. I just got more of him and more seems to feed my need for even more.

The doorman knocks on my door, which means I'm out of time. It's officially decision time and for me, that comes back to one key thing: Eric was right. I haven't told him everything and I can't. I can't look him in the eyes and tell him that I have. I can't lie to him the way everyone else has, but if I tell him everything there is to tell, his words will prove true: he'll ruin the Kingston family and that means my mother and my father's legacy along with it. I was playing with fire coming here, thinking I could stay silent. I need to just go home before I do something stupid. I let the doorman in.

An hour and a half later, I'm on a plane, and when I should be trying to decide how to move on without Eric's touch, I'm thinking about him—every touch, every kiss, every word we'd shared plays in my mind over and over again and my regrets are many. I should have said more. I should have stopped him from walking out that door, but I remind myself I couldn't. He saw too much and you don't expect a genius who sees too much to stop seeing too much. You don't ask a genius to help you see what you can't and expect him not to see everything.

By the time I'm on the ground, it's early evening, and when I walk into my downtown home, I strip down to sweats and a T-shirt, order Chinese food, and sit down at my computer. It's time to focus on what's before me. My cellphone rings with Gigi's number and I let it go to voicemail. I need a plan before I talk to her. She's no spring chicken and the idea of Eric helping us seemed to have calmed her down. I need to give her another rope to hang onto. Heck, I need to give myself another rope to hang onto. I need to hire help and that help has to be someone that can't be bought off by Isaac, and Isaac has a lot of money. I have limited resources.

My mind reaches and I grab my purse and pull out the business card I'd grabbed from Eric's desk. His cellphone and his email are on it. I pull up my email and before I can talk myself out of it, I start to type:

Eric—

I grabbed your card from your desk. I wanted to call but it felt like you were pretty finished when you left. I wasn't, but that just seems to be how things work with us.

I stop myself. What am I doing? This isn't a personal email. I should delete that. I start again.

Eric—

I grabbed your card from your desk. I wanted to call, but I thought you might welcome an email more freely. I know that your history in Denver runs deep and dark. I shouldn't have asked you to come back here in the first place, but I need someone to help me figure this out. I need to hire someone and Isaac has money and resources that I don't. I need someone I can trust who can't be bought off. So, this is me asking for help one last time. Who would you

hire to investigate Kingston Motors? Just a referral would
be appreciated and I don't even have to mention your name.
Harper

I read the message and there's more I want to say, so
much more, but I don't. I hit send and hope for a reply. In the
meantime, I start researching and looking for someone I can
hire to help me solve these problems at Kingston. I make a
list of operations outside of Denver who will be less
influenced by Isaac and my stepfather, who may or may not
be a part of what's going on. Until I know, I can't talk to my
mother. She will tell him everything.

Hours later, I lay in bed, staring at the ceiling. I grab my
phone from the nightstand, pull up my email and with the
discovery that there's nothing from Eric, disappointment fills
me. Obviously, I was just his bastard and princess conquest
he needed to get out of his system, which would make me feel
foolish if I hadn't gone into that night with him knowing that
he felt that way. He did. I knew, and for reasons I can't
explain, it felt like something more happened between us,
like there was a real connection, something lasting, but
clearly, I was wrong. It's time to move on. And yet, as I fall
asleep, I'm back in the past, living that moment by the pool
when his eyes had found me, the tingling sensation running
down my spine. The lift of my gaze and the force of that
man's attention. I've clearly never recovered.

My memory floats forward to me standing on that stage,
scanning the crowd for Eric and catching a glimpse of him
disappearing back down the path to the cottage. I'd wanted
to pull him back.

"Good riddance," Isaac had murmured next to me. "I
hope he's leaving."

And he had. He'd left. I'd felt that certainty like a sharp
knife in my chest even before I knew. And yet still, the
minute I was free of that stage, the minute the world of
people focused on my stepfather, not me, I'd hurried to
confirm. I'd walked that path toward the cottage, my heart
racing in my chest, and found the door unlocked. I'd found
the cottage empty. And I'd gone to bed, like I am tonight,
with the feel on his hands on my body, the scent of him in my

nostrils. Those piercing eyes haunting me, and the two nicknames that define our separation in my mind: the princess and the bastard.

———— ❀ ————

Eric

I'm sitting on the slate gray couch of my living room with a whiskey in my hand and my MacBook on the coffee table in front of me, that damn email from Harper open and staring back at me as it has for a good two hours. I down the amber liquid in my cup, a smooth thirty-year I need to stomach anything Kingston before I grab the Rubik's cube sitting on the table and start turning it, the numbers in my head telling stories that no one else would understand, and doing so every damn moment of my life. Right now, they're telling the story of the bastard and the princess and the numbers want the woman as much as I do.

I set the damn cube down and stand up, walking to the floor-to-ceiling window to the left of the main living area. I stop in front of the glass and nothing but inky black touches my eyes, a storm on the horizon, but out there beyond that darkness is a spectacular Manhattan skyline to kill for that I worked my ass off to earn. That no one named Kingston gave me. They don't get to give or take from me ever again. And they did take.

I press my hands to the glass, cold seeping through my palms and sliding up my arms, but there is fire in my blood, memories of the only person that could ever get me to give two fucks about anything Kingston in my mind: *Harper.*

My lashes lower, numbers exploding in my mind that become her again. That become me replaying exactly ten different moments with Harper in my arms, with me inside her, the scent of her on my skin, the taste of her on my lips.

What the hell is it about that woman that makes me need another taste? That makes me remember how she tastes? What is it about that woman that drives me fucking insane? I finally had her. I fucked her, so what if I want to do it about another twenty times? It's over. That's how it has to be.

I need help, she'd said.

My lashes lift and I shove off the window. I do not help the Kingston family.

The end.

The princess is part of their clan now, and six years deep. Helping her is helping them, and she wasn't even honest with me. There was something she wasn't telling me. She didn't even deny that truth. I sit back down on the couch and refill my glass. I don't like unknowns and where the Kingstons are concerned, that gets personal. Especially after they sought me out through Harper.

What don't I know and what consequences are there to not knowing?

CHAPTER THIRTEEN

Harper

I waste no time dressing and getting to work, and by eight in the morning, I'm in my office at the Kingston corporate offices. Today my dark hair is tied neatly at my nape, rather than loose the way I like it, a style I see as no-nonsense and all business. I've dressed in a black suit, with a pale pink shell beneath it, because I like to remind the world that I'm not one of the guys any more than I'm one of the Kingstons. I need that distinction today, and I hate that part of it is to spite Eric.

I'm *not* one of them. I need to believe this today. I'm my father's daughter, and that means I fight for what I believe in and for others. Right now, I just have to protect our customers, my mother, and even Gigi, who hasn't always deserved being saved. Maybe she doesn't now. She was horrible to me and to Eric, but seeing someone almost die and then beg for forgiveness has a way of getting to you.

I sit down at my desk and pull out my MacBook as well as the pad of paper where I wrote the different companies I want to call for aid, but I can't help myself. I power up my computer and check for a reply from Eric one last time. I actually hold my breath waiting for my email to load, only to find nothing from him in my inbox. I said I was letting go and moving on, but the enemy of your enemy is your friend. And Isaac and my stepfather have always been enemies, even when I was too naive to heed the warning Eric had given me about being used with no endgame for me but defeat.

I stand up with the intent of shutting my door, only to have Isaac appear in the doorway, and in his ridiculously expensive suit, there's no way I can avoid a comparison between him and Eric. "I see you're back to work," he says, his voice a rich, arrogant accusation as perfectly honed as his body. He's a good-looking man, his hair perfect, his jawline sharp, clean. He's refined in all the ways that the rasp of whiskers on my belly reminds me that Eric is ruggedly, perfectly male. A thought that has my cheeks heating with the memory and I cut my stare from Isaac with the ridiculous fear that he can read my mind.

"How was your trip?" he asks, hitching a broad shoulder on the doorframe, obviously planning to stay longer than I'd like unless he's going to give me the answers he's been avoiding about the recalls.

"It was a much needed long weekend," I say, hoping to avoid a topic laced with lies. My lies about why I took off of work.

"Who were you with again?"

"Don't play coy, Isaac," I say, fighting the urge to cross my arms in front of myself in a defensive move Isaac is too smart not to read. "We both know I didn't tell you who I was taking a trip with."

"And yet, I'm your brother," he reminds me, an undertone of accusation in his words. He's suspicious about the trip. I've questioned the recalls. I've tried to see paperwork he won't let me see.

"My *stepbrother*," I say, and then I dare to go to the place I don't want to go. "One who doesn't act like a brother and we both know it. Otherwise, you wouldn't have—"

"I get it," he snaps, straightening, clearly intending to shut me down before I can go down an awkward rabbit hole of unbrotherly love. "You don't want to tell me who you're fucking," he snaps. "I get it, but I want to know this isn't a distraction from your job."

"I live for this place."

"You haven't been here," he replies dryly. "And I have an issue that needed to be dealt with yesterday. You weren't here to handle it."

"I had my phone with me at all times. What issue and why didn't you call me?"

66

"I didn't call because this problem needs your full attention, and obviously, that wasn't here." He doesn't give me time to reply. "The union's bitching about the women's bathroom in the plant. I have no clue what the problem is, but it's a distraction I don't need right now. I need you to run front line on this issue—deal with them. Get them pink fucking toilet paper if you have to. They want to start negotiations tomorrow. I'll email you the details." And with that, he disappears into the hallway.

Pink toilet paper is what he wants me to handle? He wants me to negotiate with the union, which isn't my job. We have someone who's an expert in this area. Angry now, I round my desk and head down the hallway and follow him all the way toward the corner office that he calls his castle, quite literally. He disappears inside and I pass his secretary's desk, but she's not there right now. Not that it would matter. Belinda is in her fifties, quiet, reserved, and a mouse in a cat's cave who couldn't be more submissive to Isaac. That's how Isaac likes everyone.

Submissive.

He tries to shut his door and I catch it. "Why can't the union negotiator handle pink toilet paper, Isaac?" I ask, certain this is all about keeping me busy.

He stares down at me, his green eyes cool and calculating. "You really aren't good at taking orders." He leaves me in the doorway and enters his fancy office, rounding his mahogany desk, a grand mountain view and expensive artwork on the walls on either side of us because he's showy. The entire Kingston family is showy, while my father instilled humility and graciousness in my mind. Though he spoiled my mother in ways that seem to have made a showy appeal to her or we wouldn't be here now.

Isaac presses his hands on the desk. "Just do your job," he snaps. "I have a meeting in fifteen minutes."

"Since when does a member of the family, a managing member of the executive team, just do their job without asking questions?" I ask, stepping into the room without closing the door. I don't do small spaces with Isaac. I learned that lesson the hard way years ago. I stop behind a leather chair and settle my hands on the back. "That's not what your father taught me. He said—"

"The union is breathing down our throats," he snaps. "Our product is good. If we have a flaw, it's human. They don't like my attitude on this."

Finally, he's actually talking about the problem. "How can you be sure our product is good? What have we done to ensure—"

"Everything," he says. "I have this under control. Just appease the union."

"Appease the union, or stay busy and out of your hair?"

"Both, Harper," he bites out. "I have this under control. I have everything under control."

"From where I'm standing, that's questionable."

Shock runs through me at the sound of Eric's voice. I rotate to face the door to find him standing there, looking like a rebel with rumpled hair and that one-day stubble, and apparently, he left his suits in his hotel room, at least today. He's in faded jeans and a Bennett Enterprises T-shirt that hugs his hard body, his brightly inked arms in full, colorful display, his message clear: *The bastard is home. What are you going to do about it?* And when his blue eyes meet mine, they burn a path along my nerve endings, the message in their depths changes with clarity—I'm here for you.

CHAPTER FOURTEEN

Harper

I can't breathe with Eric's unexpected appearance, with the proof that he didn't ignore my email, that he didn't ignore my plea for help. He simply answered me in person, but when Isaac demands, "What the fuck are you doing here, Eric?" I'm suddenly trapped, a rat in a cage between two bigger beasts, and I don't know how to react. I don't know if this is what Eric wanted.

"Good to see you, too," Eric says dryly.

Isaac leans on the desk, perfectly manicured hands pressed to the hardwood surface. "Seriously, Eric," he says. "What *the fuck* are you doing here?"

Eric doesn't look at me. He focuses on his brother, his lips, those beautiful lips that I know to be oh-so-punishing when he wants them to be, lifting ever so slightly. "I'm family," he says, those words pure sarcasm. "Why the fuck haven't I been here sooner *should* be your question, but you know, you never call, you never write. It's really heartbreaking."

Isaac narrows his eyes on Eric and pushes off the desk, unbuttoning his suit jacket and settling his hands on his hips, his gaze raking over his brother—no, his bastard brother. "You can't afford a suit with all those millions I hear you made?"

"A billion," I say before I can stop myself. "He's a billionaire now."

Isaac's attention rockets to me. "Bullshit."

"It's true," I assure him, because while yes, I've randomly read up on Eric's successes, Gigi told me before I ever left for

Denver. "He just hit the billionaire mark." I can feel Eric's attention settle on me, heavy and sharp, and I suddenly regret those words. Now, it seems like I went to him, chasing his money.

My gaze snaps to his, the connection jolting me—my God, this man affects me. "You're very successful. That was my point."

"Was it now?" he challenges, shadows in his eyes that I do not wholly understand, but I am certain they relate to the bastard and the princess, and not in a good way. He thinks I'm one of them. He thinks I went to him with an agenda that wasn't what I claimed. He thinks I used him and now, he's here to make us all pay.

"I have work to do and so does Harper," Isaac snaps. "We'll have to have the happy reunion charade later."

Eric straightens. "Later won't work for me." He advances into the room, all long-legged swagger, to stop in front of Isaac's desk. "I've been hired to do a full audit of the company's operations and paid well enough to ensure I'm willing to spend time here."

My cheeks heat with anger and embarrassment. I'm right. He's not here for me. Gigi paid him. Of course, she did. I told her not to. I told her that changes the dynamic of his presence here. Isaac laughs. "No one paid you to audit our operations. I'm the president and my father damn sure wouldn't have called you in."

I grip the back of a chair, my only shield in the war of brothers I've never quite experienced until now. I wonder if I knew how bad it was would I have gone to Eric, but who am I fooling? I would have taken any excuse to see Eric again. I wanted that man. I still want him, even knowing now that he most likely isn't here to help me.

Eric perches on the edge of Isaac's desk, power radiating off of him as if he's just taken ownership of the entire room. "You're scared shitless that pops is up to his old games, aren't you?"

There's a flicker of something in Isaac's eyes that he quickly banks, but I saw it and if I saw it, Eric saw it. "I've earned my place here. He trusts me. So, no, asshole. I'm not afraid of anything that has your name attached to it."

"No?" Eric challenges, his hand settling on his powerful thigh, muscle flexing beneath his ink, a portion of the jaguar exposed, lines of numbers beneath it. I wonder about those numbers. I wonder if he wanted that jaguar to be exposed to mock everyone in this building, including me.

"No. We both know you rode Grayson Bennett to the bank. Is there trouble in paradise? You need a new ride? It's too late for that."

"You're not afraid of anything with my name attached," Eric repeats. "Interesting and good to know. That'll make it easy for me to get everything I need from you."

"The only thing you need from me is a kick in the ass to get out of my office. I have work to do." He swats at Eric like he's a gnat, the bastard brother, only this bastard brother is a billionaire who is smarter than him. I fight my urge to protect Eric. He can protect himself and I'm terrified that Gigi has given him the opening to destroy us.

"You'll get him *whatever he wants.*"

At the sound of Gigi's voice, I turn to find her standing in the doorway, and at five-foot-one with flaming red hair and piercing blue eyes, she might be seventy-seven, but she's a force to be reckoned with. "You underestimate me, boy," she snaps, her voice loud, but Isaac shakes like her hands. "I told you I need to know what's going on," she adds, curling her fingers into her palms. "You told me to rock away in my rocking chair, which by the way, I don't own a rocking chair."

"Grandmother—"

"Gigi," she amends. "I'm Gigi around these parts, the woman who started this place, like Harper's father started her family's business. Now let's get real for once. Either there is something going on you don't want to tell me about or there is something you don't know. Your brother will figure it out."

"No," Isaac says in instant rejection. "No, he will not. There's nothing going on here but normal business. You will not disrupt our operation. You're getting old and paranoid."

She snorts. "Not old enough to suit you. Eric gets his brains from me." She looks at Eric. "Didn't know that, did you? I'm smarter than the average gal, despite the fact I let Grayson Bennett steal you away from us." She doesn't give him time to reply. She homes in on Isaac again and orders, "Get him what he asks for, son. Don't make this more difficult than it has to be."

"You don't have the power to make this call," Isaac argues. "I know you did this while dad is in Europe for a reason, to sideswipe me and root Eric in my business before he could stop you, but he's one phone call away and our combined stock overrules yours."

"Actually," Eric says dryly. "My stock with Gigi's combined overrules any vote."

"You don't own stock," he snaps.

"I do now," Eric counters. "I bought out the bank this morning with a premium they couldn't resist."

Isaac goes completely, utterly still and I watch as hell swims in the depths of his stare. "You did *what?*" he bites out, while I swallow hard at this unexpected turn of events that might just change this company forever, and I'm not sure it's for the better, not when I see the real anger between these brothers.

"Family needs to be protected by family," Eric says, his gaze shifting to Gigi. "Don't you think, Gigi?"

Now she swallows hard, a telltale sign that she had no idea he'd done such a thing. "Yes," she says. "And I haven't always remembered that, son. I do now."

"So, Harper tells me," he says dryly, eyeing Isaac, "I'll work in the conference room for now. Get me access to all databases and all facilities."

"That will take time," Isaac says.

"I'll get it done myself," Eric says. "I'm impatient like that." He looks at me, his blue eyes sharp, but unreadable. "You'll work with me on the audit. Everything else will come second. It was one of my terms when I agreed to do the audit." Perhaps it's my imagination, but I swear that his voice lowers, the heat in his eyes smoldering with possession as he adds, "You're all mine."

CHAPTER FIFTEEN

Harper

I'm burning alive under Eric's scorching attention, melting right here in the center of Isaac's office with the message in his burning blue-eyed stare: he came here for me. He also promised to finish this family off if he returned. Maybe that means he intends to fuck me in every possible way this time. I don't know. I just know that as seconds tick by, our present company of Isaac and Gigi fades away and there is just the two of us and a challenge that I don't understand, but I'm certain I will soon.

"I'll leave you three to get this done," Gigi says, snapping me back to the room just in time to find her exiting the office.

"Go do your job, Harper," Isaac snaps at me. "Eric and I need to have a conversation alone."

Eric's lips twitch, his eyes never leaving mine, nor mine his. "I'll find you when we're done," he says, and there is this heady possessive undertone to those words that is anything but professional. This is a promise that we still have unfinished business, that we are far from done, and I have never felt so owned in my life. Considering this place, this family has made me feel pretty darn owned, that's saying a lot. It's different with Eric, though. He owns everything around him. He owns me. He's different from Isaac and the rest of them in ways that connect with me on every level. I *crave* this man's confidence. I *need* this man's touch. I *understand* this man's hunger for revenge in ways that he can't know, and yet, I fear that very need in him is why he's here, is why he's now dangerous.

"You can leave the door open," he adds, his tone sharpening with a swift change in mood as he refocuses on his brother. "Isaac and I won't be long."

The air crackles and this time it's not about me and Eric. It's about him and Isaac and that snaps me out of my lusty haze and shoots me straight into fight mode. My gaze shoots to Isaac. "He's here because Gigi wants answers. I tried to tell you that. I asked and asked you to help me give them to her. You dismissed her as an old lady and forgot how much power she has. So, suck it up and just give Eric what he needs. Give Gigi what she wants." I look at Eric. "As for you. You aren't a bastard because he calls you one. You're a bastard if you choose to be one." I look between them. "We're family whether you two like it or not. You need to figure this out."

I march for the door and exit, Eric's voice following me as he says, "She has no idea what kind of bastard I really am, now does she, Isaac?"

That statement, layered with history, halts my steps and I lean on the wall waiting for more. What does that even mean? I need to know what that means and I wait for an explanation, but the door shuts. I'm shut out. Damn it. I push off the wall and hurry down the hallway, reaching the elevator just as it closes, no doubt missing Gigi by seconds. I cut right and take the stairs, rushing down the winding path until I reach the bottom level just as the elevator doors open.

Gigi steps out and pauses to smooth the red dress she's wearing, oblivious to how the color clashes with her hair, which is more orange than red. "I expected you before I made it to the elevator," she says, cutting me a look, her blue eyes so like Eric's in this moment that I shiver. "You're late," she adds and starts walking toward her office, which is the only office down here by her design.

"That wasn't exactly neutral territory you left me in," I say, easily catching up to her despite the fact that she's remarkably spry for her age. "And you know I don't like you down here. You don't even keep a secretary. What if something happened to you?"

She waves me off the way Isaac tried to wave off Eric and with the same failed results. "I'm fine down here. This is the cave, no men allowed." She glances at me before entering her office, "Eric's quite the looker these days, isn't he?"

My cheeks heat and she laughs. "You noticed." She disappears through the doorway. "And I noticed the spark between you two."

Of course, she did. "And you," I say, swiftly changing the subject and following her inside what is more a small executive apartment than an office, "should have warned me about what just happened."

"And you," she counters, "should have told me when you left New York City. He called me."

"And you offered him how much money?"

"Enough to get him here."

"He's a billionaire now," I say. "He doesn't need your money."

"He damn sure took it," she says, pointing at the chair next to her. "Sit."

I ignore the order, stopping in front of her, my hands on my hips. "He didn't need that money," I repeat. "He took it because he could make you pay him. Because he hates you that much. He's now got stock. He came here to destroy us."

"And you really think that if he would have come without the payday, he would have had another motive?"

"He's here to take over," I say because it sounds better than his promise that his return would be to "finish us off."

"Better him than someone else," she shocks me by saying. "At least then I'll die with this place in the hands of someone who's blood, someone who will make it thrive. We don't know what is going on, but we know it's bad. This is my legacy. I don't want it to end in jail."

"Gigi—"

She holds up a hand. "He's brilliant. He'll save your father's legacy along with mine. Go. Work. Get him what he needs. This is what we both wanted. Eric here, finding out what's wrong. We got it. Now he's here."

"For the wrong reasons," I say.

She purses her lips. "We'll see. He wanted to be a part of this family from the day he met his father. We didn't make him feel like he belonged. And understandably after that, he needed a reason other than that need to be here now. Money, and even revenge, serve that purpose. Now go. Keep an ear to what's happening."

I could fight with her, but that achieves nothing obviously and I really do feel a need to be back upstairs, but she's dismissed my stepfather in all of this. "Your son—"

"Jeff will suck it up and deal with it, just like you. Go."

I give up, at least for now. I turn and head for the door. "Harper?"

I turn to face her. "Yes?"

"I love you, honey, and you've been there for me this past year, but when I tell you to do something, you do it. This is still your job. We both know I gave you instructions where Eric was concerned and you ignored those instructions."

She's right. I did. I didn't want him back here this way for reasons I'd point out, but she won't listen. I nod and exit the office, a million emotions clawing at me, but I show none. Emotions are used against you in this place. My need to protect my mother and even my father's legacy is why I'm still here. That need is an emotion. It's trouble, like Eric, and I can't seem to walk away from that combination.

Eager to be in my own space, where I can privately melt down and then stand back up and fight, I hurry up the stairs. The doorway to my office is like sweet relief. I enter my office and I've made it all of two steps when I hear. "Hello, princess."

I whirl around to find Eric in the doorway and he doesn't stay there. He shuts the door and starts walking toward me, the look in his eyes as predatory as the jaguar on his arm, and like all prey, I'm thrust into a moment where I must make a decision to stand and fight or run. And I am prey. His prey, and before I can make a move, he's standing in front of me, that earthy male scent of him seducing me.

"We're not done yet," he says. "Just in case you hadn't figured that out by now."

CHAPTER SIXTEEN

Harper

I have about thirty seconds to process Eric's declaration that we're not done before he pulls me close, all that sinewy muscle absorbing my body, that powerful edge that is this man, owning me, and he owns me all too easily. I try to resist. I know I'm the enemy to him. My hand settles on his chest but I'm not sure if it's to touch him or push him away.

"Eric," I whisper, and I feel the charge radiating between us, the heat, the ten shades of lust that come from deep, dark places for him and for me; they just exist, because he exists.

He tangles his fingers in my hair, and lowers his mouth to mine. "We are definitely not done yet," he repeats, the words almost guttural and then his lips are on my lips, his tongue stroking long and deep, stealing my breath and driving away everything but how he tastes, how he feels; that's how easily I'm lost and found in this man. It's doesn't matter that he could very well be the one to destroy us. Not in this moment, not when he's kissing me, not when I get that one last taste of him I've wished for these past hours, but it's not a kiss that he allows me to drown in, it's not even a kiss that lets me swim in the moment.

He tears his mouth from mine, his lips a warm breath from another kiss that I hunger for in ways I didn't know any man could make me hunger. "I'm here now," he declares. "Just like you wanted."

His touch, his taste, his very existence in this room is burning me alive, but so is the hate between him and this family, *his* family. "This isn't how I wanted you."

One of his hands slides up between my shoulder blades, molding me close. The other caresses up my waist, cupping my breast, sending a wave of sensations through my body. "How did you want me, Harper?"

My lashes lower and I pant out a breath. How did I want him? Too many ways. So many ways. "Impossible ways," I say, trying to tear away from his grip, but he pulls me back to him, that damn earthy scent of him driving me insane, consuming me the way he's threatening to consume me. The way he already has in some ways for six long years.

"Let go," I growl. "Let go *now*."

"What impossible ways?"

"Without the hate. You can't be here and not hate."

"Is that what you think? That I hate you?"

"The bastard and the princess. You said it. I felt it in that hotel room. You wanted to punish me."

"I wanted a lot of things in that hotel room. I still do."

"You don't even deny it."

"Did I want to spank you? Yes. Did I want to fuck you hard and fast and do it all over again? Yes. Did I want to fuck you out of my system once and for fucking all? Yes, I did. But I failed. I failed and now I'm here." He maneuvers me to the desk and presses me against it, his big body caging mine.

"Stop. You hate me. I'm not fucking a man who hates me again, but apparently, I am going to get fucked by him in all kinds of ways. I should've never asked you for help. And yes, you're a bastard, and not by name. I told you. You claim that with actions."

"What haven't you told me, Harper?" he demands, wanting information with me as a side order.

"We're not finished, you said?" I challenge, hating that I melt for him when he has an agenda, hating even more that I opened the door to that agenda. "You mean you're not done using me?"

"Who's using who, princess? You came to me."

"I didn't use you. I'm *not* using you, unless a request for honest help is now considered using."

"No?"

"No. And you just kissed me to get information."

"I kissed you because I couldn't fucking help myself, and for the record, I don't like what I can't control."

"You hate me. Stop kissing me."

"I don't hate you, Harper. I hate secrets and lies. What aren't you telling me?"

"Like Gigi didn't tell you? I know she told you." I shove at his chest, a sudden need to have the clear head his body touching my body won't give me.

His hands shackle my hips, the touch scorching, possessive. Controlling. "Tell me yourself."

"I was supposed to offer you money. I didn't. I refused."

His eyes narrow, lips thin. "And why exactly didn't you offer me money?"

"You don't need it."

"Is that right?" he asks, sounding amused.

"Yes, it is. You don't need it, but that wasn't the point. The point was that the man who came here for money, came here for financial gain, not to help his family."

"These people are not my family. *You* are not my family."

I recoil as if slapped. "I know how you feel about me. I get it. I just told you that. That princess thing is all about reminding me that we're divided."

"We're only divided if you're with them."

"I'm trying to make my way, just like you did, Eric, but my mom is here and she's made foolish decisions. That doesn't make me love her less, though. If it were your mother—"

"I'd have gotten her out."

"You think I haven't tried? She's a fool for your father and for the record, I fucked you. I kissed you. That doesn't mean I can't think beyond an orgasm. I won't be a fool for you like she was for your father." I shove on his chest. "Get off of me. Get back."

"Is that what you really want? For me to back away? For me to get back on a plane and go away?"

"Like you'd do that now? You bought stock. You decided to take over."

"You don't take on a Kingston without leverage. I made sure I had leverage. To help you. You asked for help. I'm here. So, let me repeat this," His hands settle on my face, his voice softening, "I came *for you*."

Heat sears the air between us, a hot flash of desire fueled by how good we are naked together, by how much we really aren't done with each other. "I'm afraid to trust you."

"Good," he says, pulling back to look at me, wicked heat in his eyes. "I haven't earned that trust."

"I haven't earned yours either," I say, and it's not a question. "And I never will."

"If I wasn't willing to see beyond this family, I wouldn't be here."

"You're here to ruin them, and me with them."

"From what I've seen, and I've seen far more than Isaac thinks I've seen, you didn't need me for that. I could have sat back with a bag of popcorn and watched the fun."

Realization hits me. "You came because you knew you could take over. It wasn't about saving us. It's about getting what you always wanted."

"Princess, I haven't wanted or needed this place in a long time. I got out and got right like you should have."

"I couldn't. I told you that. I told you why. I would have left the legacy behind, if not for my mom. Seriously, what if it was your mother? Would you just leave? I don't know why I'm telling you this."

"Because you want me to be human enough to care."

"Are you?"

He cups my face. "Enough to bow to a princess, it seems." His voice is low and raspy as he leans in and brushes his lips over mine and then suddenly he's kissing me, drugging me with his tongue, before he says, "Decide what you're going to do with that power, Harper. Then I'll decide what I'm going to do with mine." He strokes his thumb over my cheek. "I'll see you soon." He releases me and in a few, graceful strides, he's out of the office, and I'm alone. Only, I'm not sure I am alone anymore.

I'm with him, I'm with Eric, but I'm not sure if he's my friend or my enemy. I just know that if that man touches me, I'll melt, and I won't care if that means pain or pleasure.

CHAPTER SEVENTEEN

Eric

Harper's like the apple in the Garden of Eden, tempting me in ways that I simply can't resist. I know she could be poisonous. I know she could be playing with my head, but I still want her and in a wicked, fierce way. I want her so fucking badly that I'm here at Kingston Motors in a building I swore I'd never step foot in. The taste of her. The feel of her against me. The sweet floral scent of hers that clings to me as I exit her office, a distinctively *her* scent that's a giveaway to how that conversation behind closed doors went just now: up close and personal, the only way I want things with Harper.

I won't hide that fact from her or anyone. That's not my style. I want. I need. I take and I never shy away from announcing that intent, nor would that benefit Harper, considering her present position. With the way my appearance went down, she's officially placed herself inside a war zone. More so, she's declared herself standing on my side of the battlefield, and for that, she'll pay without my protection. Isaac will come at her with that desperate viciousness I know all too well, just as he knows where that leaves him with me. He needs to know what that means with Harper.

In fact, there's no reason to play this on the lowdown with Isaac. I'm halfway to the lobby when I turn around and walk my ass back to Isaac's office. His door is shut but I don't care. I open it and step inside. He's standing at his window, his phone in his hand, with his back to me. He whirls around and his expression reddens the way it had every time our law profession pitted us against each other in mock trials.

"I need to call you back," he says to whoever he's talking to before he disconnects the line. "Knock, you little bastard," he snaps. "You might be performing an audit, but I run this place."

"Last I heard, your father still ran this place. Good to know who's responsible for its current state of destruction. I won't keep you. I have data to dissect. I just want to be clear. Harper's a pawn Gigi used to get to me. If you use her or lash out at her, you'll suffer, and as in the past, when I make a promise I keep it."

"No matter what you have to do to make me pay, right?" he challenges. "I thought Grayson Bennett and his ever talked about moral compass would have changed that in you."

"I operate based on who I'm dealing with and we both know you don't even understand the words moral compass. Leave Harper out of this."

"Harper put herself in this. She wants the company." He leans on the desk. "Smarten up, brother. She's brought us together for a reason. We just don't know what it is yet, but I promise you, at its root, it's about power. It's about how damn much she thinks her father contributed to this company."

"Last I heard, she's the one who contributed and with no stock to show for it. You have her trust fund."

He gives an amused snort. "I didn't know you were so fucking naive," he says. "She has no trust fund. Her father left it fluid and under her mother's control. She wants you to take me down so she can take over. She wants what's mine and assumes as the bastard, it will never be yours. Believe me, man, she'll fuck you up and down and sideways to get what she wants."

He hits a nerve I didn't realize still existed about this company, this life, and even the woman I came here to help, but I beat it down. "What you fail to understand, dear half-brother, is that I don't want or need this place. If she takes it from you, I'll be amused. This isn't my life."

"Then why come here at all?"

"We're family," I say dryly. "Harper said so."

"That's why you wear the jaguar, a competing emblem, inked on your arm? Because we're family?"

"That's exactly why. It's all about family to me."

"If that's family to you, you're ten more shades of fucked up than I even realized."

"I have a feeling we'll be reinventing how we define family and fucked up many times over before I leave." My lips quirk. "Harper works for me. Remember that. You need her, you come through me." I turn and exit the office, cutting left and down the hallway. I've just cut right when I end up toe to toe with Harper, who all but runs into me.

I catch her shoulders, and holy fuck, touching this woman sets me on fire, muddying the water in ways that I allowed to pull me into this hell. "Hi," she says softly.

I narrow my eyes on her, thinking about her six years with this family, thinking about what it takes to live like one of them that long. "You wanted me here. You got me. You work for me now. You report to me now. Put together any data you think I need to see and don't make any move related to that data, and I mean *any* move, without talking to me first." I release her. "I'll be in the conference room." I turn away and head for the front office, but I don't make it far.

"Eric," she calls out, and my name on this woman's lips easily halts my steps, but I don't immediately face her. For a moment I'm back in that hotel room with her naked, in my arms, me buried inside her when she used my name and told me that she saw me, not the bastard. I wonder who she sees now. I wonder who she really saw then. My jaw clenches with that thought and I turn around to find her stepping in front of me, the small space of the narrow walkway shrinking and wrapping us in intimacy.

"I don't know what I sense in you right now," she says. "But remember this: Isaac has trashed you every day of your life you've been connected to this family. You think we're different, but he sees me just like he sees you, and he is not kind to me. I deal with it. I handle it, but to you, we're different. To him we're alike."

"And to you?"

"In some ways we are. We both got forced into this family and we both wanted it to be a real family. I, however, wasn't smart enough to get out of here like you did when I could have, but I was smart enough to ask for your help. Because the way I see it, doing nothing wasn't an option. If you take everything, then at least I'm finally free." She turns and walks away and I watch her disappear into her office, the damn floral scent of her every-fucking-where, the way I want her naked in every fucking thought. Which would be fine if that nerve Isaac hit wasn't jumping again.

I came here for her.

He knows it.

She knows it, too.

That's only a problem if there's something going on here, and my gut says that it's designed to fuck me over. I don't know why I'm a target, but I am, and if Harper knows the truth, she's going to tell me, even if I have to strip her naked and cuff her to my bed to get it out of her.

But I'm still not sure she does. I'm not sure that she's not being used or even targeted herself.

A thought that I can't quite materialize claws at my mind, the way so many do until I realize them, until I turn them into numbers that no one but me can understand. I need to be alone and think. I also need Harper naked and cuffed to the bed, but that comes later. Not much later. *Tonight.* It happens tonight when I decide if I trust her or I just want to fuck her.

CHAPTER EIGHTEEN

Eric

With a vow to have Harper naked and in my bed tonight, I turn on my heel and walk into the lobby where I stop in front of the receptionist, a pretty blonde I'd guess to be in her twenties—and knowing Isaac, his fuck buddy. That's what he does. He surrounds himself with pretty women who place him on a throne and kneel in front of him. A thought that has me remembering Isaac's comment inferring Harper would fuck me to get what she wants, though her fucking me for any reason suits me just fine. Now, if she fucked him, that would be another story, and a really fucking bad one I'd have a hard time believing.

The receptionist eyes the back office where I just exited and then me again, obviously trying to figure out how I got back there without her knowing. "Can I help you?"

"I'm Eric Mitchell, the other brother."

Her eyes go wide and then as often is the case, they rake over my tats, and then sharply lift. "You're—as in—"

"The bastard?" I ask, but I don't have to wait for her reply. I get right to the confirmation. "Yes. I'm him and I'm a stockholder called in on behalf of Gigi to audit the operation. I'll be working in the conference room, if I have calls or deliveries or if anyone simply wants to share operational concerns."

The phone rings and she looks awkward, like she's not sure if she should do her job and answer the phone. "Answer it," I order. "I'll wait."

She swallows hard and picks up the phone. "Kingston Motors, can I help you?" Her eyes go wide. "Mr. Kingston.

85

Yes." She looks at me. "He's standing right here. Yes. Of course." She punches the hold button. "He wants to talk to you."

"Conference room," I say, heading to the left of the desk toward a set of stairs that will lead to a lower level opposite Gigi's private domain. Gigi, who might have convinced Harper that she's a new woman, but I know better. She has an agenda, something she's after, something I can give her, and she's smart enough to know I'll find out what that is and she's willing to take that risk.

I take my time going down the stairs, aware that my father could have called my cellphone. He called the office phone to record my reply, or allow Isaac to listen in, or both. Once I'm at the double glass doors of the lower level, I open them to enter the massive conference room, where I head to the end of the mahogany table and grab the phone, punching the line. "Father," I say, though that word is acid on my tongue.

"I understand you're now a stockholder." His tone is dry, unaffected, but then he enjoys games, and while I don't, we're smack in the middle of one.

"I never pass on a steal of a deal. I got it cheap. Those recalls haven't been kind to your stock or apparently your cash flow."

"Our cash flow is just fine."

"Considering you had to sweep Harper's trust fund out from underneath her," I say, "I imagine it is."

"Sweep her trust fund?" He laughs. "That's a joke. You don't know half the story, boy, but you will. I'm on a private jet about to head home. We'll talk and I promise you that even that genius brain of yours will feel enlightened." He disconnects and I lean back in my seat. *I don't know half the story.* He's right for once where I'm concerned. I don't know half the story, but I'll know it all soon.

My cellphone rings and I snake it out of my pocket to find Blake's number on the caller ID. "Talk to me," I say, answering the line.

"There are cameras and recording devices in the room you're in, which from what I can tell has been the case for years."

"Of course," I say dryly, finding the idea of my brother recording people and using those recordings against them—me included if I give him the chance, which I won't—highly probable. "What else?"

"About fifteen minutes after you left your brother's office, the tech team for Kingston Motors suddenly began deleting chunks of data; which even dumb shits like me that don't have your genius IQ can assume is to hide damning information before you gain access."

"Only it's too late to matter."

"Exactly," Blake confirms. "I have everything downloaded as planned for comparison. I'll send you a secure data file that homes in on exactly what was deleted. It'll take a few hours once they finish what they're doing to finish the analysis on our side, but it'll allow you to see what matters, which is what's now missing."

"That's going to be an interesting study."

"Even more interesting, we've hacked all cellphones, emails, and external communications. Isaac somehow called his tech team and your father without me knowing when he did it, which tells me that he has a phone line or device that we don't know about."

In other words, he was operating off the grid before I walked in the door. "There's a person I wanted you to focus on," I say, redirecting the conversation to where I want it: Harper.

"You wanted to know where Harper fits into the family hierarchy. She doesn't. She's not close to any of them. She isn't even close to her mother anymore. Word on that is there's tension between them, perhaps over the trust, though Harper still sees her twice a week. Outside of that, she doesn't socialize with your brother or father."

"Not now," I say. "What about in the past?"

"We've gone back two years. She's been removed from the family for at least that long."

"And yet she's still here," I comment, half to myself. "What about Gigi?"

"She has more contact with her than the others, but I'd still call it limited."

"Then there has to be someone else. Who?"

"If you mean love interests, we're already working that angle, but on first glance, there are only two men she's dated over the years. They're both rich, powerful and involved with your father and brother. However, that doesn't raise a red flag to me necessarily. They were in and out of her life and inside her normal social circle. That's who she'd be exposed to, and gravitated to, naturally."

Rich, powerful, men. The kind I wasn't when she met me. The kind I am now. I could let my head go all kinds of places, but I don't. My mind jumps from there to my father's comment about Harper's trust fund.

"I'm texting you a question when we hang up," I say, focused on discretion. "I'm also about to grab my computer and set up here in the office. I'll be waiting on that data."

"Don't do that," he says. "The cameras are too wide-sweeping. Take your ass out of that place. I'll find you a sweet spot in the building by tomorrow."

"Find it right here in this room."

"They'll know you had it swept."

"Works for me."

We disconnect after a few more words that amount to not much and I send the promised text: *There could be more to the trust fund than meets the eyes. Look deeper.*

Once Blake confirms receipt of the message, I reach in my pocket and start turning the mini Rubik's cube inside, processing all that I've just learned, playing with the numbers in my head. I abandon the cube and stand up, ready to ask questions around the facility. Ready to see Harper. I'm almost to the doors when they open and she enters. We now stand a few steps apart, the charge between us combustible. The two of us in the same room is like a match to a flame.

We stand there, staring at each other, the air thick, that charge all but lighting us up and I, for one, say fuck it to the family drama. I'm thinking about her naked on this

88

conference table, and if we wouldn't become Isaac's nightly porn viewing, that's exactly what I'd make happen.

Her lips part as if she knows where my head is and she cuts her gaze. "Do you need something from me, Harper?" I prod.

She swallows hard, that long, elegant, regal throat of hers that needs my mouth, bobbing before she looks at me, her stare unwavering. "Need? Yes. I need. *To talk*. And to give you this." She holds up a file in her hand. "This is—"

I shake my head to silence her. Her brows knit and she tilts her head, realization seeping into her intelligent stare. She knows we're being watched and I close the space between us. "I'll take that," I say, that sweet scent of her teasing my nostrils again, my cock twitching, blood heating.

She offers me the file. "You wanted my schedule," she improvises. "I didn't have your email, so I brought you a hard copy."

"Good," I say. "Because you're all mine now until I leave."

"And when exactly will that be?" she asks.

"When I get what I came for," I say.

"And what's that?"

I lean in close and lower my voice. "More. I came here for more."

Her eyes jerk to mine and her reply is rapid fire. "Define more, because, under the present circumstances, I'm not sure how I feel about that word."

"I plan to and in great detail," I assure her. "I'll look at your schedule. We'll discuss where that leads us."

Her lips press together, and I can tell she's biting back words before she settles on, "I have questions."

"As do I, but now isn't the time for the answers we both want, and in fact, demand."

"When?"

"Tonight," I say.

"I'm not sure that works for me," she says.

"I'm certain you can make it work. If you can't, I promise you, I will. I think I've proven that."

"No, you haven't," she says, anger radiating in her voice. She grabs my arm and leans in close, her voice low, a whisper for my ears only. "I didn't get naked with you to get you to come here, and I won't do it again to keep you here. I didn't pay for your services, nor is any version of the word 'more' a given." She leans back and looks at me. "That you think it is, is arrogant, and frankly, a bastard-like assumption that I don't like."

That comment smacks like a palm. "It's what you expect, right? Why would I disappoint?"

"It's not actually what I expect. Not from you. Not at all." With that, she turns and leaves me standing there, staring after her, hot and hard, and ready for more, however we define that word.

CHAPTER NINETEEN

Harper

I don't know what just happened, is all I can think as I enter my office and shut the door, letting my mind chase answers now that I'm alone. The first thing that comes to my mind is: *That man.* My God, that man. Eric is making me crazy. I want him. I'm angry with him. And we're really being watched? Am I being watched now? That idea jolts me and I push off the door and walk calmly to my desk. If Isaac had turned into a peeping tom, I'm not giving him an emotional show for him to use against me or Eric for that matter, despite the way he just treated me.

Yes, Eric just acted like that bastard label he too readily owns, but considering the power play at hand, I can't say I blame him. I don't have his trust. He doesn't quite have mine, but after talking to Gigi, I don't know if it matters. She's right. We're better off in Eric's hands than Isaac's. Even if I lose my trust, which at this point feels pretty gone anyway, at least I leave this place without liability, and so does my mother.

I hope.

I don't know.

Eric could burn us, but I just don't feel like he will. Not unless he feels that we're trying to burn him. I think that's exactly what he thinks. He thinks I fucked him to fuck him. I want to scream with this idea. I want to go right back down those stairs and shake him and quite possibly get naked with him. How can I want to be naked with a man who basically accused me of being a whore? Okay, that's extreme. He didn't exactly say that. I'm exaggerating and I don't usually exaggerate, but he's making me crazy. And confused. I've always been confused about that man, or at least, emotionally. My body feels no confusion. It just wants to feel him close.

The intercom on my desk buzzes and the receptionist announces, "Jim Sims from the union is on the line for Isaac, but he told me to give the call to you."

Jim Sims, who would do about anything for me if I got naked with him, which is exactly why I don't deal with him. Isaac knows this. He doesn't care, and this isn't even about Eric, considering this was my assignment before he knew Eric was here. It's about me asking too many questions and making too many demands for answers. Which wouldn't be a problem if Isaac wasn't hiding something.

I pick up the line. "Jim."

"I hear you're lead on the upcoming labor relations topics."

"I hear that as well. I was just about to catch up on the file before tomorrow's meeting."

"Yes, well, we both know bathroom preferences are below your pay grade. I suspect your brother hoped you'd distract me and calm me the fuck down on some of the bigger financial issues."

"What issues?"

"A topic better discussed in person. Let's meet."

Of course he wants to meet, and to be all touchy-feely while he's at it. I glance at my clock. It's eleven. "How about three o'clock at your office? That gives me time to get up to speed."

"How about happy hour, at the wine bar up your direction in Cherry Creek? You still live in Cherry Creek, right?"

How does this man know where I live? "Yes," I say. "I'm still up that direction."

"Good. These matters are easier stomached when diluted by wine and you won't have far to travel after we indulge."

"I'm not good with wine," I say. "I need a clear head today and tomorrow. Let's stick with the coffee."

He's silent a few beats and then says, "Then we'll do coffee at five. I have meetings this afternoon."

We disconnect and I pull up my email to find an email from Isaac titled "Union" that I skip right on past when I see one from EricB@kingstonmotors.com. I hit the email and read: *My new email. Just to make my presence official.*

My brows furrow at the "B" that most certainly stands for "Bastard" and I type: *Did you choose that email address?* And then hit send.

His reply is instant: *I never let anyone else make my decisions. You shouldn't either.*

I ignore his obvious reference to my reasons for staying with Kingston for six years and type: *Did you really make it Eric B, for bastard?*

He replies with: *There's another Eric in accounting. I didn't want anyone to get confused. Here's my phone number. Use it. Often. 212-415-2333.*

I grab my phone and check the number to the one I got from his business card, and it matches. I send him a text: *Now you have my number.*

He replies with: *I already had it, princess.*

I stare at that message, not sure if we're talking about phone numbers or that conversation downstairs about me fucking him to get him here. I suddenly don't know if I should be angry or not thus I have no idea how to reply. Yes, I do. I type: *And I already had your number as well, BASTARD.* I stare at the message and erase the BASTARD. I replace it with *ERIC.* He doesn't get to hide behind the bastard persona with me. He gets to own every asshole moment.

I pull up my email and click on the entry from Isaac to read: *Make the union happy. The last thing we need in the press right now is a union scandal.*

He says nothing more. He doesn't even sign the damn thing. I grimace and download the union files. The list of issues they want to negotiate stretches well beyond a bathroom and I have a gut feeling this is about keeping me busy. That was his plan before Eric got here. Get me so entrenched in union hell that I didn't have time to look at him and his handling of the company. He played that card too late. Eric's here and one thing I'm certain of, he's not leaving until "this" whatever this is, is over.

I move to my conference table and set up my MacBook, and settle into reading the union data. Two hours later, I have pages of notes on a legal pad, with nothing in here that our labor relations manager couldn't handle. There is nothing that would become a problem for the company and yet me blowing it would certainly be a reason to dispose of me from the company. Is that what this is? A set-up to get me out? It's such a paranoid, insane idea that I toss my pen down and stand up. I need food and out of this office.

I head to the break room for a cup of coffee. That and a power bar will have to be my lunch. I've just finished doctoring my cup to perfection when Isaac appears in the doorway, hitching a shoulder on the doorframe. "He's not family."

"He's more family than I am. He's blood, whether you like it or not." I march toward him, trying to force him to move. He doesn't. "I need to get back to work."

"You brought him here to take what you want. He's going to take what he wants. Those two things won't connect."

"You assume you know what I want," I say. "Because you assume everyone wants in the same ways you do."

"You assume you know what Eric wants."

"No, I don't," I say. "I asked him." I leave out the part where what he wants is to destroy this place.

"And he said what?"

"I'm not going to pretend to have any right to speak for Eric. Ask him yourself. Now. I have a meeting with Jim to prepare for, and for the record, I know you know that man is all hands and this is torture for me. Now you have the satisfaction of confirmation, but if you think I'm going to screw this up because Jim is pawing at me and give you a chance to push me out, you're wrong."

He studies me for several beats. "Perhaps you should treat me the way you treat our bastard brother, and ask me what I want, rather than assuming."

"What do you want, Isaac?"

"Just what's mine and now you've made me have to fight for it, and if it gets bloody, that's on you. It didn't have to be that way. It wasn't that way."

The words cut and accuse and I don't know what to do with them or what to feel. He steps out of the break room and pauses a moment, glaring to his right before he turns and disappears left. I know even before I enter the hallway that Eric's standing there.

I suck in a breath, preparing for the impact of his presence, and then he's replaced Isaac in the doorway, big and broad, with all that ink and muscle everywhere but next to me. I want him next to me again, and it doesn't seem to matter what he might think of me if that happens. His eyes, those crystal perfect eyes, meet mine—no they crash into mine, and seem to grab hold of me, deep inside and hold on.

"This isn't on you," he says, stepping closer, lowering his head near mine. "He's responsible for every decision that drove you to me." He pulls back to look at me. "And later tonight, ask me what I want again." With that, he turns away and exits the kitchen.

CHAPTER TWENTY

Harper

At four-thirty, I pack up my briefcase and contemplate calling Eric, or at least texting him, to tell him I'm leaving. He declared himself my new boss and on that, there is no argument to be had. The silence since that claim, however, is disconcerting, and I'm feeling generally confused about what he and I are doing. I head for the lobby, let the receptionist know that I'm leaving, and exit the building into the chill of a November day. Quick stepping as I dig my keys from my purse, and click the lock on my Kingston vehicle and wonder what it would be like to have the freedom to drive something else. I try to remember my early years here when I was all about the brand.

I'm about to cut between cars to my door when a car pulls up next to me, and I hear, "Get in."

At the sound of Eric's voice, I turn to find the passenger window down on a black F-TYPE Jaguar and him inside it, causing my heart to flutter. When has any man but this one ever made me react in such a way? I force a tiny breath, which is remarkably hard to draw in, and walk to the open window where I lean in and find those blue, blue eyes of his fixed on me.

"Get in," he repeats.

"I have a meeting," I say. "That union thing I was talking to Isaac about. I'm on my way there now."

"I know. I'm going with you."

He's going with me? Do I want him to go with me? Yes. No. "The thing is," I say, "you can't go with me. The union contact wants a one on one with me."

"To grope you and make you miserable. I get that, which is why I'm going with you. Now, get in."

He wants to protect me from being groped? I want to be protected from being groped. "If you come, he'll be difficult."

"I'm good with difficult people," he assures me. "I had a year of practice with this family which for all their faults, have served me well."

"You're in a Jaguar."

"Quite the statement car, don't you think?"

"Like your ink?"

"Like sending the princess to bring the bastard home."

"That's not how that played out," I say.

"No?"

"No," I say.

"Get in the car and tell me."

"We make Kingstons," I counter. "Let's take my car."

"For the love of God, woman. Would you just get in?"

"Fine," I breathe out. "I give up. I'll get in." I open the door and he grabs my briefcase and sets it in what little backseat there is in this version of Jag. "A hundred-thousand-dollar F-TYPE," I say, claiming the seat next to him, the earthy, clean scent of him teasing my nostrils. "Impressive ride considering you just got into town." I reach for my seatbelt which doesn't want to move. "Well, except for the seatbelt." I yank hard and Eric catches the belt halfway across my body and the two of us end up holding it, a warm blanket of intimacy surrounding us.

"The dealer warned me that the belt can snap back," he explains softly. "I wouldn't want you to get hurt."

But I will, I think, and not by a belt or this family. By him. He will steal my breath and own my body, and then leave. I can't stop it. I don't think I even want to try. He slides the clip into place, his hand intimately brushing my hip as the belt snaps together, but he doesn't move away. His eyes sharpen. "You have to be careful with shiny, new things. They look pretty but sometimes they bite."

He's not talking about the belt or the car. He's talking about me. He's telling me he doesn't trust me and yet he's here.

He settles back in his seat and places the car in drive while I decide that I'm back to generally confused with this man. "Starbucks, right?" he asks.

"How do you know where my meeting is being held?"

"Anything you say in that building is being monitored."

"By you?"

"As of today, yes, but that place has been wired to the hilt for years from what my people can tell."

My heart lurches and I rotate to face him. "My office?" I ask urgently. "Are there cameras in my office?"

He pulls us to a halt at the exit to the parking lot and glances over at me. "Yes. Your office."

I hug myself and face forward. "I change for the gym in there a few times a week. I don't even want to think about what that means." He pulls us onto the highway and starts the short, two-block drive to the coffee shop. "I don't know if the idea of Isaac or your father watching me freaks me out more."

"I wish I could comfort you, but I'm the bastard child of a father who was having an affair."

I press my hands to my face and then drop them to my legs, thinking back over the years. "Isaac is the one recording me," I assert. "Your father doesn't see those recordings. I'm certain of it. Isaac uses them and me. He's always a step ahead of me. He knows what I'm going to do before I get to do it. He claims every big moment I attempt. Your father always ends up impressed with him and disappointed in me. He steals my ideas."

"Once a cheat, always a cheat," he says, pulling us into Starbucks. "That's his way. That's how he beats you."

He's right, I think as he parks the F-TYPE. That is Isaac's way, and yet I've foolishly played this game his way all this time. Eric kills the engine and I turn to him. "He didn't beat you. Everyone knows he didn't beat you. You came out on top, better off than him. I know that doesn't come without personal consequence for you, Eric. I know asking you to come here was selfish, but I need you. We need you."

"Because he didn't beat me," he repeats.

"Exactly. He didn't beat you. He *can't* beat you."

His jaw sets hard. "Right," he says flatly, that word, his only reply, holding about ten thousand meanings I want to understand. There is so much about this man I want to understand. I wonder if anyone really knows him. I wonder so many things.

"Eric," I say, a million possible words playing on my tongue when my cellphone starts ringing in my purse. I ignore it and focus on him, taking a chance, and assuming I might read him right. "I hate that you might think me needing your help translates to me using you like they would. I'm not them. I wanted—more." My cellphone finally stops ringing.

He shifts to face me, the full force of his piercing blue eyes on me now. "More," he repeats.

"Yes," I whisper. "More."

My cellphone starts ringing again.

"Take the call," he says softly.

"I don't want to take the call," I say. "I want you to talk to me."

He surprises me then and reaches up, his fingers brushing my cheek, a light touch I feel everywhere, and I want everywhere, sending a shiver down my spine. My phone stops ringing and starts all over again. His hand falls away. "Take the call, Harper. It could be your union groper."

"He is a groper and yes," I reluctantly agree, "it could be him." I grab my phone to find my mother calling, no doubt about Eric. "It's my mother," I say, sticking my phone back in my purse. "I'll call her back."

"You sure?"

"Positive." My phone starts ringing again. "She goes for three," I explain. "After that, she leaves a voicemail."

He studies me a few beats, something dark and unreadable in his stare, but I don't need to read his expression to read his thoughts. He knows I don't want him to listen in on this call. "Look," I say. "She probably found out that you're here. She's going to be a freaked-out mess, afraid of you, and pissed at me. I really don't care if you hear that call, but it's going to be painful and long." It rings again. I grab it from my purse and hit decline before sending it to voicemail. "Eric—"

"Don't let me find out you're lying to me, Harper." His voice is low but hard. "That's a broad statement so let me repeat and expand on it. Don't let me find out that you lied to me about anything."

"I'm not," I say, looking him in the eyes, letting him see the truth. "I swear to you, Eric. I'm not lying to you about anything. There are things I haven't told you, but not because I don't want to tell you. I just haven't had the time or privacy."

"I seem to remember things differently."

"You mean the night you told me the only way you'd come back was to finish off the family?" I challenge.

"I didn't come back to ruin them," he says, his blue eyes watching me closely as he adds, "I came back for you."

He's here for me.

Those were the words I'd wanted to hear from this man, but now that he's said them, they're layered with complexity, the meaning holding a world of possibilities, some good and some not good. "That could mean a lot of things," I say.

He leans in closer, his hand on the back of my seat. "What do you want them to mean?"

CHAPTER TWENTY-ONE

Harper

He came for me.
I want to know what that means to him.
He wants to know what that means to me.

Eric lets those questions linger in the air between us and he's so close, so very close to me, his hand on the back of my seat, his face so near my face that I could reach up and trace every handsome line. "I wanted you to come here, and yes, I wanted you to come for me. But I also never wanted you to leave, not from the cottage or the hotel room, but you did. Easily. You walked away without looking back, so it's hard for me to believe that you came for me without another agenda."

"I left and you stayed. For six long fucking years, you stayed with them. And Gigi sent you to me. I could easily believe that you have an agenda."

"I told you my agenda. I need your help. I don't want to be your enemy, Eric."

"I'm only your enemy if you make me your enemy."

"I won't. I chose a side when I went after you."

"Gigi's side?"

"My father's, and my father would have respected you for all you've done on your own. He would have despised Isaac. You're not him and I'm not her, that person you made me, we're not the princess and the bastard."

"I told you," he says, reaching up, his knuckle brushing my cheek, sending shivers down my spine, "I'll make you like that name."

I catch his hand. "And you like being the bastard?"

His gaze lowers to my mouth and lifts. "I am who I am, Harper."

"Well, I'm *not her*," I say. "I'm not on a throne. I'm not above you because I inherited money I don't even have, or because I'm my father's daughter, or whatever the case."

"I'm here. Stop obsessing over a name."

"How can I not obsess over that name? I was in that hotel room with you when you were calling me that name. I felt the anger in you when you used it."

"Not at you, Harper."

"Now who's lying to who? I was there. Let me repeat myself. *I felt* your anger. You hated me for being a part of this family."

"And yet you fucked me?"

"Right. I did." My throat constricts, hurt and anger colliding, and yet my voice is remarkably calm. "I must have wanted something. I get it. That's what you think of me." I turn away from him to face forward.

Eric doesn't move away. He stays right there, leaning over me, watching me. "Harper," he says, his voice low, rough. "That's not what I meant."

"It doesn't matter," I say, my skin tingling with the need for him to touch me. How can I need a man to touch me? How can I need *this* man, who hates me, to touch me?

"It *does* matter," he says. "*You* matter or I wouldn't be here."

I want to believe him. I want to touch him. I want him to touch me. I want him to kiss me and I know he will if I turn to him. I know I'm setting myself up for heartache with this man. I know he could use me, but I'm so damn drawn to him.

"Look at me, Harper," he orders softly.

"I can't or I'll forget you hate me." It's at that moment Jim exits Starbucks, his long legs eating up the parking lot in a near run as he charges toward his car. "That tall, dark-haired man is Jim," I say, glancing at Eric, and reaching for my seatbelt. "He's the union guy. He's leaving." I let my belt fall away. "Why is he leaving?" I open my door and climb outside, the cold contrasting all the heat Eric and I were just generating and I shiver as I call out, "Jim!"

He looks my way and I swear it's like he's seen a ghost. He keeps walking toward his car, a Mercedes that says he's paid well for his negotiation skills he isn't using right now. I chase after him, certain now that somehow this meeting was Isaac setting me up for a fall. "Jim, wait," I say catching him at his door. "I thought we were meeting?"

"I have a situation," he says, scrubbing his jaw. "I can't meet with you tonight."

Eric steps to my side. "Hi, Jim," he greets, and it feels familiar, like they know each other.

"Eric," he bites out. "I just heard you were back in town."

"I noticed," Eric says dryly.

Jim's lips thin and he looks at me. "I'll see you at the meeting tomorrow." He opens his door.

"I thought we were talking through the hot points?"

"I told you," he says, pausing with his hand on his door, "I *can't* meet."

"What about in the morning?" I press, confused by this change of attitude.

"I'll see you at the meeting," he replies, cutting his eyes and disappearing inside his car. His engine revs and he's backing up in sixty seconds flat.

I turn to Eric. "What was that?" I demand.

"The Bennett Corporation operates one of the largest law firms in the world. We've had a few thousand dealings with the union."

I shake my head in instant rejection. "No. No, he was afraid of you. He knew *you*. He feared you."

"He fears the beast that is the Bennett name and I'm a large part of Grayson Bennett's brand."

"There's more to what just happened," I say, a cold gust of wind biting through me, while Eric seems immune to anything real. He doesn't even seem to notice. He's colder than I thought. He's harder. Why didn't I know this? He's a self-made billionaire. That doesn't come cheap. "You said you want more from me," I say. "You demanded more of me, and yet all you're giving me is accusations and a blow-off answer to something that directly affects me." A few people walk out of the coffee shop and I lower my voice. "You want more.

Well, I want more, too. I *demand* more." I start walking to the car and I even manage to get the door open.

Eric catches my arm and pulls me around to face him, all that hard muscle and warmth touching me everywhere, and Lord help me, that's where I want him. Everywhere. I want him so badly it hurts, even though I know that he's going to hurt me. "You want more?" he asks, his voice a low, rough command.

"Yes," I say without hesitation, some part of me aware that this moment defines us, it defines me in a way I do not yet understand, and yet, my answer is unchanged. "Yes," I repeat, barely able to breathe with the jagged edge of his emotions suffocating me.

"Say it," he orders as if he thinks I can't or won't. As if he needs to know I know what I'm agreeing to, and I do.

"I want more."

His eyes glint fire and ice in the same moment, still managing to burn me alive. "You sure about that? You might not like what you find if I give it to you."

My hand settles on his chest, his heart thundering under my palm. We're not talking about Kingston. We're talking about me and him. "I don't want you to just walk away this time."

"You should. You don't know who I am or what I am."

"And if I want to find out?"

His mouth closes down on mine, his tongue licking into my mouth, a deep, drugging stroke followed by another before he whispers, "Get in the car, Harper."

CHAPTER TWENTY-TWO

Harper

Eric releases me and I am instantly cold again where I was warm moments before, and I want to be warm again, the kind of warm that I know from experience only his touch creates in me. I climb into the car, letting the soft leather absorb my body. He shuts me inside and in a few moments, he's here with me, the implication of what just happened between us, and where it leads, expanding and consuming us and the small space we share. The promise of more is with us, and I don't even know what that means. I just know I need to know. I need to know now because this man does that to me. He makes me need and want on a level I don't even understand.

I just do.

He doesn't immediately turn on the car. He sits here next to me, staring forward and there is this sudden shift in energy in him that I can't explain. I feel it even before he looks at me, and asks, "Are you hungry?"

Am I hungry? Not, are you lying to me? The question settles easily between us, the tension of moments before uncurling just that easily. This is new territory for us. We have never shared a meal or a real conversation and I am quick to welcome such a thing. "Yes, actually, I am. I had a power bar today. That's all."

"I had a bag of peanut M & M's which I promise you were better than the power bar. Let's go to Cherry Creek and eat. I know you live there and it's also where I booked my hotel and not because I'm stalking you. It's my old stomping grounds and I wanted to revisit some of my favorite spots while I'm here."

"I didn't know you lived in Cherry Creek. How long?"

"Four years. I went to undergrad school around there. My favorite Italian restaurant is there, which is on my list of places to hit while I'm here."

I perk up. "North?"

"North," he confirms. "You like it?"

"Love it. My favorite, too."

"Is it?"

"It is."

We have this moment of connection then, that isn't really over North or Cherry Creek, but rather us. Just us and that drag between us that refuses to be ignored. "Then North it is," he says finally, revving the engine and backing us up. "How'd you end up in Cherry Creek?" he asks once he's driving us through the parking lot.

"I went to a lunch there with my mother when I first moved here and fell in love. It reminds me of home."

"New York City?" he asks, pulling onto the highway.

"You've read up on me," I say to the reference of my home state.

"I did," he says, offering no apologies or explanation.

"Is there a file I can get on you?"

He casts me a sideways look. "I'm right here. Just ask me."

"As if you're that approachable."

"I am," he says, glancing over at me again. "Tonight, I am."

"Why tonight?"

"It's time." He doesn't give me a chance to ask what that means. "Why does Cherry Creek remind you of New York City?"

"We lived in a tiny pocket of the city there. Everything we wanted was in a small space. Cherry Creek is like that in that everything is right there, within reach, minus the smog, rats, and crush of people. It's quaint and safe, hidden from the rest of the city in so many ways."

"It's the hidden part I liked," he says. "It's like a small city boxed off from the rest of the city."

"So, after your undergrad, you went off to Harvard?"

"Yes. And then I went off to Harvard before joining the Navy. And yes, that's a complicated story." He turns us into the Cherry Creek neighborhood. "And yes, you can ask me about it while we eat."

"I will," I say, "and actually, I live two blocks from the restaurant. You can park there if you like. Though, I guess if you're at the Marriott, North is practically next door."

"I am at the Marriott, but I'll park at your place." He doesn't ask me where I live. He just cuts right and then left and pulls into the driveway of my gray-finished house, then around to the back. "The address was in your file and I have a photographic memory."

I look at him. "As in literally?"

"Yes. Literally." He opens his door. "I'll come around to get you." He exits the car and I hear the trunk pop. I open my door and by the time I've settled my legs on the ground, he's in a sleek black leather jacket, and pulling me to my feet and to him.

He shuts the door, and I end up against the car with his hand on the side of my face, this warm, intimate blanket surrounding us, consuming us. There are no lies, no doubts, no divide. There is just this crazy, hot connection we've always shared. "I'm going to have to kiss you now, Harper." His mouth comes down on mine, his tongue pressing past my teeth in a slow, deep stroke that has me gripping his jacket and leaning into him.

He pulls back, his mouth just a breath from mine, lingering there before a band seems to snap between us and we're kissing again, and this time he doesn't hold back. He kisses me deeply, completely and when I whimper with just how much I need more, he pulls back. "Let's go eat, sweetheart. We need to talk and we won't talk if we walk in your door."

"Sweetheart? Not princess?"

His hands go to the lapels on my trench coat. "You were right. I use it to divide us. No more princess."

"Why? What changed?"

"You hit a few hotspots back there in the car. This place makes me too like my father and my brother. I'm not the me I know as me now when I'm here. They taught me to distrust and attack. The SEALs and the Bennett family taught me to reserve judgment and give people the benefit of the doubt. I prefer that version of me."

"Meaning me?"

"Yes." He strokes my hair behind my ear. "You. Definitely you, but I don't trust my judgment with you, Harper. I'm too invested."

"Invested?"

"You know I am or I wouldn't be here."

"You have a lot to be invested in here that isn't me."

"Nothing I want to be invested in *but you.*"

"But you—"

"Left. I know. And as I said, I'm here now. This time is different. I feel it. Don't you?"

"Yes, I do. Despite you being angry at me. I feel the difference now."

"We'll talk about my anger. We'll talk about a lot of things." And with that coded promise, he wraps his arm around my shoulders and turns me toward the front of the house. "Let's go get that pasta."

He sets us in motion and we walk in what is surprisingly comfortable silence, but my curiosity about this man gets the best of me. "I'm surprised someone with your academic capacity stayed here for school. Why not Harvard all the way?"

"I got into some trouble when my mother was sick. We had money issues and I shoplifted. It fucked up my academic history."

I'm stunned at this confession and I want to ask about it, but we've reached the door of the restaurant. He opens the door for me and we're greeted by a hostess that takes our coats and promptly escorts us to a half-moon-shaped booth. I slide in one side as Eric goes to the other and when I think we'll sit across from each other, he scoots all the way around and pulls me close, his hand on my leg. "This okay?"

"Yes. This is good."

"*Good.*" His voice is a low rasp, his eyes warm and reluctant as they leave my face and focus on the waitress. "Let's start with drinks." He looks at me again. "You do like wine, right?"

"Love it. Red, white, and trying new variations."

"Then I'll order my favorite here and you can tell me what you think." He gives the order to the waitress and refocuses on me. "Do we feel like enemies, Harper?"

"You never felt like my enemy. And if you think taking over the company makes me see you as that, it doesn't. The only thing that makes you my enemy is if you turn on me or my mother."

"Your mother is aligned with my father."

"I know. I've tried to get her to see that we have real problems, but she's is blinded by love. I feel like there's something illicit going on. She's not involved, she's just not helping to solve the problem. So, I'm asking you to please keep her out of this."

"I will," he says, his fingers brushing my cheek, sending a shiver down my spine. "You have my word."

I reach up and catch his hand. "Thank you," I say, a wave of heat between us and I think there is something real between us, something that isn't fantasy sex and "what if" but real.

"Your wine has arrived," the waitress announces and we linger together, seconds passing before we turn our attention to the waitress who hands Eric a sample of the wine and waits for his approval before filling our glasses.

Once we're alone, I sip the wine, a sweet yet oaky flavor touching my tongue. "It's excellent," I say.

"Glad you like it."

I set my glass down. "About that anger."

He sets his glass down on the table and his hand slides under my hair, settling on my neck. "I'm angry at you for making me want you so fucking bad that I had to come here."

Those words are raw and real, vibrating along my nerve endings. "Are you going to make me regret it?"

"There are many things I want to make you feel, Harper, but regret is not one of them."

CHAPTER TWENTY-THREE

Harper

Eric presses his cheek to my cheek and whispers, "Do you know how badly I want to take you to the bathroom and fuck you right now?" Heat pools low in my belly as he pulls back to look at me and adds, "Or anywhere, for that matter?"

My body melts while my mind fights for reason. I can't end up naked and confused again with this man and in no different a place than we are now. "Which would be fine if you could do it without hating me along with the rest of the family," I say, my hand pressing to his chest, the other landing on his tattooed arm as I place more space between us. "I'm not them. Do it the Bennett way, not the Kingston way, and judge me for me."

The waitress chooses that moment to reappear and say, "Okay. Just had to deliver another order. Are you two ready?"

Eric studies me several beats before he asks, "Do you know what you want?"

"Yes. Spaghetti and meatballs. You?"

"I do," he says, glancing at the waitress. "The same for me."

The waitress asks a few questions and then she's gone. Eric's attention is immediately riveted to me. "I *want* to know your story, Harper, not theirs."

"Do you? Because you seem to think you already know it. I dreaded the idea of you thinking I thought because we'd slept together I could manipulate you in some way. You walked away from me without looking back. What power could I ever have over you?"

"You were the only one in this family that had a chance to get me here, and you knew that."

"Because I'm not them. Not because we slept together. You have a file on me, but files don't tell you the real story. Not about people."

"Then you tell me."

"Are you going to really listen?" I challenge.

"I assure you, sweetheart, no one has ever had my full attention more than you do now, for about ten different reasons. *You* tell me *your* story." He rotates to fully face me.

I do the same of him. "And you'll tell me yours?"

"I already started telling you my story. You know far more about me and my life choices than I do yours."

A story of lies, secrets, and pain that I push aside. I focus on what matters right here and now. The part of my story that I hope he understands. "I was close to my father and his heart attack pretty much destroyed me, but my mother was such a mess that I somehow found a way to step up and be strong. I was close to my mother, too, until we joined this family. She was a young mother, seventeen when she had me, and instead of dividing us, it brought us closer together. But since she married your father, there's been a slow divide."

"Why do you think that is?"

"I know why. It's because I push back and fight for what I think is right in the company, more so this past year when I felt that there were things that didn't add up. I felt that even before the recalls. That pushback has not been well received. My mother just wants me to appease your father and brother."

He leans in closer. "What don't I know?" he asks, those blue eye glinting with intelligence. "You said you needed time and privacy, but that there were things you hadn't told me."

"You already know I'm aligned with Gigi. That was the thing I dreaded telling you the most, but I told you. I knew I needed to tell you."

"Aligned?" he asks, his entire mood darkening. "How fucking aligned?"

I reach out and grab his hand. "Not against you. I swear to you, Eric. I don't believe Gigi is fully repenting for her sins.

I believe she's worried about losing the company. She doesn't want her legacy to go down in flames."

"You do know that I hate that woman enough to want to burn it to the ground, right?"

"You said you came for me, not her."

"I *did* come for you, Harper."

"Then please, I beg of you, don't burn it to the ground. My father's world was half that company."

"Your father is gone. His legacy is *you*. You don't need that place."

"So you're going to ruin Kingston?" I try to turn away and he pulls me back around.

"No," he says. "I'm not going to ruin them. I don't need to do that. I don't need them at all."

"But you thought you did. You told me that in the past."

"I had a need for family after I lost my mother and the Navy filled that void. I came here to Denver the night I met you because I'd lost that connection. I thought I needed family but these people were never family."

My gaze goes to one of the tattoos on his right arm, a black and gray skull with an anchor that I assume represents his years as a SEAL. My hand dares to settle over it, our eyes locking, warmth waving between us. "Harvard graduate. Genius IQ. Navy SEAL. Self-made billionaire. You are so many things that this family is not."

"This family will kill you to get ahead. My fellow SEALs, and anyone with the Bennett name, that's real family to me, the kind that would bleed to protect you."

"Then you understand family, despite this family. You protected your mother. You understand why I stayed for mine. I know you do. You say you don't, but you're not seeing me and the real picture. The company is all I have left of my father and my mother—I *love* her. She might not be perfect, but she's all I have."

He inhales and cuts his stare before he looks at me again, his eyes turbulent, a story in their depths that I don't understand but want to understand. "I understand why you were here. I don't understand why you're *still* here, though."

"My mother—"

"Is my father abusing her? Is she in danger?"

"If there was negligence that was intentional, there's criminal liability that she could get wrapped up inside. I could end up with that liability, too. You know Isaac will look for a fall guy. I'm terrified. I can't leave now. *I* could end up the fall guy."

"Have you done something to expose yourself?"

"No. Not that I know of, but who knows what fingerprint I could have on something I don't understand. I don't know what's happening. I just know something is. The recalls. Weird money movement."

"You need to be honest with me."

"I am. I am being honest with you."

"What don't I know?" he presses, and I want to scream with the impossibility of this situation.

"I already answered that question. I can show you everything I have collected, the paperwork, the notes I've taken. The information Gigi gave me. I have it at my house."

He tangles his fingers in my hair, and drags my mouth to his, obviously oblivious to anyone else around us. "If you burn me, Harper, you won't like the results."

"What can I do to make you trust me?"

"We need to leave."

"Why?"

"Because I'm here for you. I came for *you*. I want, and can, protect you but you aren't being straight with me."

"I am," I whisper. "Stop saying that."

"I say what I see, sweetheart, and clearly," he adds, "the only way I'm getting everything from you is with your clothes off. I need to talk to you and I need to fuck you and I can't do both here."

Heat rushes over me. "You don't have to get me naked for me to talk."

"Let's do it anyway. Any objection to that plan?"

"No," I whisper. "No objection."

CHAPTER TWENTY-FOUR

Harper

After announcing that he's basically taking me home to fuck me, Eric kisses me, a deep slide of his tongue that is over too soon, but he doesn't pull back. His lips are a breath from mine, lingering there, taunting me with another kiss that doesn't come, and the sound of the restaurant buzzes around us, fading away. The intensity of the pull between us stealing my breath. "Holy hell, woman," Eric murmurs, stroking my hair and then lifts his hand to flag the waitress.

That stroke of my hair undoes me. It's intimate. It's possessive and tender, a command and a question. No man has ever made a simple act so very provocative. No man has ever affected me like this one. He's ruined me for anyone else and that's a little bit terrifying.

The waitress joins us and Eric is quick to get us out of here. "We need boxes," he says. "We'll take it all with us."

The woman looks confused. "Oh. Yes. Of course."

"Quickly," Eric adds, impatience to his tone that he makes up for by adding, "There's a big tip in it for you."

Her eyes go wide and she rushes away. Eric immediately leans over and brushes his lips over mine again. "You taste like trouble."

"I wish I weren't," I say, my eyes meeting his, "but we both know I am."

"Yes, but trouble suits me, sweetheart. Wait and see." He winks and my stomach flutters. God, how he affects me with the smallest of acts.

The waitress re-appears and in a few quick minutes, our food is boxed up, wine corked, and the bill paid, all the while

I'm thinking about his comment about trouble suiting him. Once we're ready to go, we both stand and the minute we're on our feet, Eric laces his fingers with mine and leads me through the restaurant. With each step, I can feel the swell of need between us. We pause at the door to grab our coats and Eric helps me with mine. That simple act is intimate, the air around us charged.

We exit to the street and he pulls me under his arm and aligns our hips. We start walking, neither of us speaking for a full block, a mix of sexual tension and unspoken words between us. A push and pull of lust and need with questions that need answers. It's then that this connection I have to Eric, *with* Eric, drives home another feeling. I have so much guilt where he's concerned.

I stop walking and turn to face him, the dim lighting of the cozy little neighborhood now mixed with the beam of a bright full moon. "I don't want to be trouble for you, Eric."

He cups my face. "I told you. I'm good with trouble."

My hands go to his face. "I was selfish asking you to come. I know what Gigi did to you and your mother. I'm sorry."

"And she's doing it to you, too," he says. "You just don't see it."

"At least she wants what I want," I say. "That's where my head is. I can't do this alone. I've tried. I can't get answers from Isaac or your father. I got shut out."

"You have me now."

"Because I pulled you in. Because I didn't let you just do what you wanted and stay gone."

"I did what I wanted," he says. "I came here for you. I wanted you. I *want* you. I need to trust you, though, Harper. I don't like your connection to Gigi."

"I know that. I've been honest with you about it. And I need to trust you. I don't care what your plan is if it saves my mother. Take the damn company. You're right. I'm my father's legacy. I don't recognize Kingston as anything he was anymore."

"Deep breath, sweetheart. Better things are coming. I promise you. You know what I need to do for you right now?"

"Do for me?"

"Yes. Do for you. What you did for me the night we met. Fuck this damn family out of your head."

"Is that what I did?"

He lowers his head, his lips near mine, breath a warm fan on my cheek. "And a lot more, sweetheart, or I wouldn't be here now." He brushes his lips over mine. "Come on," he says, turning us back onto the sidewalk.

This time, we have a short one-block walk and everything but that need between us fades into the wind. There is something happening between me and this man, and it's not just sex, but it drives that need to be intimate between us. My skin is flushed. My sex has clenched just thinking about being naked and in Eric's arms again. We turn down my drive. "Back door," I say. "I always go in there."

We close the space between it and us, that combustible need between us, just that, combustible. I unlock my door and we enter directly into the kitchen, white stone beneath our feet. I flip on the light, illuminating an island in more white stone, and cabinets a slate gray wood wrapping a half-moon-shaped room. I slip off my coat and set it on a barstool, turning to face Eric as he shuts the door and locks it, before setting the take-out on the counter to his right. He shrugs out of his coat, his T-shirt stretching over his broad chest, before he drops it on a stool next to mine, his eyes never leaving me. He steps into me, aligning our bodies, and I feel the heat of him. I feel the change in us. This isn't a power play. This isn't us climbing walls to get to each other. The dynamic between us has shifted.

His hands frame my face. "I nicknamed you princess because you were so fucking beautiful and regal standing there by the pool that night."

"I wasn't regal," I say. "I don't want you to think of me that way."

"In a good way, sweetheart. This is me telling you that you had me before hello."

It's everything I want to hear from this man, perhaps too much. "Did you know it was me? Did you know who I was?"

"No, I didn't."

119

"I knew it was you. I'd seen pictures."

"And?"

"And I knew I should stay away," I admit.

"Why?"

"That whole forbidden, taboo stepsibling thing. And all the hate between you and the family."

"And yet you still came to the cottage?"

"You made me mad."

"Let me make it up to you," he says, his mouth closing down on mine, a deep slide of tongue undoing me. I moan and that's all it takes. We are crazy, wild, kissing, his hands sliding over my waist, over my hips, cupping my backside. I tug at his shirt, desperate to feel warm skin over taut muscle. Desperate to feel him. He tugs my skirt up and that's when my doorbell rings.

We both pull back. "Expecting company?" he asks.

"No. No one visits me."

He pulls my skirt down and strokes my hair again. "Get rid of whoever it is."

I nod and hurry down a hallway that leads to the front door. I peek through the curtain to find my mother standing there. "Oh God." I rotate to find Eric in the hallway.

I close the space between us as my doorbell rings. "It's my mother," I say softly. "She's going to go off on me about you."

He arches a brow. "You want me to leave?"

"No, I want you to stay, but I don't trust her not to repeat everything to your father."

"You want to save her but you don't trust her?"

"She's not logical with him."

"I'll choose my words with that in mind."

"Sorry about this."

He cups my head and kisses me. "Make it up to me."

I smile. "I will," I promise, and I love that he's being so easygoing about this.

I hurry back to the door and open it. My mother is standing there, looking stunning and far younger than her forty-six years, her ivory skin pale perfection, her black pantsuit sleek and elegant, her dark hair in waves around her shoulders. "Why haven't you called me back?" she demands.

"Come in, mom," I say, backing up to allow her entry.

She steps into the foyer and her eyes lock on Eric. "What the hell is he doing in your house?" she demands and then looks at me. "Don't you know why he came here?" She looks at Eric. "I know why you're here."

CHAPTER TWENTY-FIVE

Harper

"I know what you're doing," my mother snaps at Eric again, and my God, she charges at him so quickly that I barely have time to put myself between them.

"Mom!" I shout urgently, my hands catching her arms. "Stop. Stop it right now."

"Why is he here?" she demands. "Why?"

"If you mean why is he in my house, it's because I invited him. If you mean, in general, the same answer applies. I went to New York. I found him. I asked him to come here."

"Then you're a fool. We are the ones who have something to lose, and he has everything to gain."

Frustration and anger shorten my patience. "He's a billionaire, mother. He doesn't need anything from this family."

"He's not a billionaire."

"Yes," I say. "He is."

"It doesn't matter what he is or isn't. *We* are your family. He is not."

That pisses me off. Now, she's doing what the rest of this family has done to Eric and that's not the person I know. She doesn't hurt people. "*He's* family. He's a Kingston. He's blood. We aren't. Don't act like them. You're not one of them."

"We *are* them," she says, driving home every accusation Eric has ever made toward me.

"We are *not them*." And because I don't want her to say anything else to hurt him when this family has done nothing but that, I turn to face Eric. My hand settles on his chest, my

123

need to touch him, to let him know that I'm with him, not them, absolute. "I'm sorry," I say, my eyes meeting his, my hope that he sees the truth in my words, in all that I have told him, in them.

"There's nothing to be sorry for," he says softly.

"Yes, there is," I say, wishing he'd touch me. I really want him to touch me, especially since I know I have to speak to my mother alone to get her to see reason. "Can you give us just a minute?"

"Of course," he says, his tone and stare unreadable, that hardness that is so a part of this man, back and etched in his handsome face. His blue eyes cold, ice I know is meant for the Kingstons, and now I'm a Kingston to him again. I hate that ice. "I'll be in the kitchen," he adds.

"Don't leave," I whisper urgently, my fingers closing around his shirt and I don't care if my mother hears. I add, "Please. Her words are not mine."

The ice in those eyes of his, warms, the hard edge of his mood softening as he covers my hand with his. "I'm not going anywhere." He tightens his grip. "Let me know if you need me." He releases me and turns to walk down the hallway.

"Are you sleeping with him?" my mother snaps at my back with Eric still within hearing distance. Honestly, I'm fairly certain he will hear everything from the kitchen anyway.

"That has nothing to do with this," I say, whirling on her.

"That's not a no. You are."

"He's helping us. How about being glad that he's that kind of man? That he actually came here to help."

"He didn't come to help. Your father says—"

"My father is *dead*. Gone. And your husband is letting everything he worked for, including your future, get wiped away. You could go to jail."

"We are not going to jail. No one did anything wrong."

"You could actually," I say. "People died, mother. If there were choices made that ignored risk to human life—"

"Stop," my mother says now. "Stop right now. That didn't happen."

"And you know this how? Because even Gigi is scared. She wanted Eric here."

"Gigi hates him."

"Gigi was afraid of him when she should have embraced the one person in this family that has his shit together."

She closes the space between us and actually grabs my arm, lowering her voice. "Gigi treated him horribly," she whispers. "I didn't know he was a billionaire, but I knew he was powerful. He'll try to take everything. Don't let him use you to do it."

"Don't turn him into the monster. People didn't die on his watch."

"You don't know what you're diving into here," she warns. "You have no idea."

Those words come with such conviction that I narrow my eyes on her. "What aren't you telling me?"

"There's nothing to tell," she says. "You're creating problems that don't have to exist. My God, Harper, fuck him out of your system and send him home. Please. I beg of you."

I feel those words like a slap. My mother doesn't say things like that. Ever. "What aren't you telling me?" I repeat.

"I have done nothing but love you and take care of you and so has this family. Treat us like it."

"This family has done nothing for me. You are another story. *You* are my family. I'm trying to protect you."

"You're trying to ruin my life. Your father—"

"Stop calling him that. Please."

"Jeff," she bites out. "He's not pleased that it's my daughter that brought this problem to his door."

"He's a solution, not a problem, and one day you'll thank me for this. And I hope you'll thank Eric as well."

"Get rid of him. I beg of you. No. I order you. End this tonight." She turns and opens the door and exits, slamming the door behind her.

I stand there and the room seems to weave around me. I'm trembling, I think. I don't tremble, but my mother is my world. She's all I have and she's never talked to me like this, but Eric—he's the one helping her and me. It's then that I dare to admit that he matters; he's the guy that could hurt me. He's the one that I could trust and be burned alive because I did so. He's that guy for me. He always has been.

His footsteps sound behind me and I turn to find him standing in the archway. We stare at each other, the room weaving again but this time with this crazy connection I share with this man, and questions between us again that I don't want to exist.

"Could you hear it all?" I ask.

"Yes," he says, his expression unreadable still, but he closes the space between us, stopping a reach from touching me but he doesn't. He doesn't touch me. "I could hear everything," he says. "What do you want right now?"

My hand presses to his chest. "You. I want you."

"You want to fuck me out of your system?"

"I tried that. It didn't work."

"Do you think I'm here to hurt you?" he asks.

Tension crackles between us. My body aches everywhere he's not touching me. "No, I don't. And I hate that she acted that way. I hate the things she said to you. I know they hurt you. I know you could hurt me because they hurt you but I can't seem to care. I know we're just fucking, but—"

He drags me to him, his fingers tangling in my hair. "Sweetheart, if we were just fucking, I wouldn't be here." His mouth closes down on mine, his tongue stroking deep, and I feel it everywhere. I feel this man everywhere. I want him everywhere and I need him to know that and more. I just need and need with this man.

I press my hand to his chest. "Eric—"

"Harper," he murmurs. "Forget what just happened. We're here. We're now. Be in the moment with me."

We're here. We're now. Something about those words both pleases and taunts me in a strange combination that I never get the chance to understand. He's kissing me again, drugging me with the taste of him, spicy, male, demanding, and suddenly he's scooping me up and walking under the archway toward the living room.

The next thing I know, I'm on the couch on my back and he's coming down on top of me, his legs aligned with mine, his hands at my face. "Ask me what I want, Harper." His voice is this low, raspy seduction that is both silk and satin on my nerve endings.

"What do you want, Eric?"

"You," he says, "from the day I met you. You. I've fucking wanted you, but you were the enemy."

"And now?"

"And now this," he says, and then his mouth is back on mine, warmth spreading through my body, consuming me the way only he can. He does. He consumes me. It's terrifying. It's addicting. He's addicting.

What do I want?

More.

Him.

More of him.

And despite it perhaps being the definition of insanity, I know there will be a price to pay, but I don't care what he costs me.

CHAPTER TWENTY-SIX

Eric

There is something about this woman that burns through me like sunshine on a winter's day, warming even the cold of this city, this family. She is *why* I'm here. Hell, she's always been in my fucking head, burning me with memories of touching her, with wanting her. I mold her close, drinking her in, the taste of her on my tongue, the scent of her—a sweet floral spice—wrapping me in the spell that is this woman. She cast a damn spell on me at the pool the night we met, one that time and space didn't erase.

"Not a princess," I murmur against her mouth. "A witch."

Her fingers curl on my jaw. "*Not a princess. A witch.* What does that mean?"

I roll her to her back. "It means," I go to my knees and pull her upright with me, yanking her jacket down her shoulders to hold her arms captive, "you cast a damn spell on me or I wouldn't be here."

"No, I—"

I kiss her, my tongue stroking away her objection before I say, "You did or I wouldn't have thought about you for six long years."

"You thought of me?"

"Yes, Harper, I did and I resented you for it. For that power over me."

"I thought of you, too. Let go of my arms. Please, I want to touch you."

There's a part of me that doesn't want to let that happen. That doesn't want the crazy way she affects me to steal my damn control, because she does. No one else can, but she absolutely does. There is something in her voice, in her eyes, a vulnerability, a need I haven't sensed until tonight. A vulnerability I know comes not just from my ability to affect her situation. It's about her mother. It's about how painful I know that conversation she just had with her was, and I get it. My mother and I had so many fights driven by the family. I lost her and though Harper's mother doesn't have cancer to drive a suicide like mine did, Harper is still worried about her safety.

I kiss her again, the taste of her, the feel of her, is sweet honey on my tongue that I've craved every day since I left it behind. "You, woman," I say when I tear my mouth from hers, and just barely touching my lips to her lips.

"You," she whispers. "You. *Eric.*"

Eric.

She's telling me she sees me, not the bastard. "Harper," I whisper, making sure she knows I see her, not them. I stand up and she follows me, this tiny, feisty, beautiful woman. She tosses her jacket and kicks off her shoes. I turn her and unzip her skirt before sliding it and her panties down her hips and lifting her to kick them away. I drag her blouse over her head and toss it. My hand goes to her belly, pulling her to me, while I unhook her bra and then cup her breasts, holding them in my hands. She leans into me, her backside pressed to my cock, my fingers tugging at her nipples. She moans and I bury my head in her neck, inhaling that sweet scent of her, just breathing her in. I've never done that with any woman but this one. I never wanted to savor a woman instead of fuck her. I want both with Harper and I don't even know what to do with that.

Fuck. She's dangerous and I can't seem to walk away.

She's in only thigh highs now, and I press her to her knees on the couch, placing her backside in the air, and I stroke my hand over her hips, my cock throbbing, but it's so fucking much more with this woman. My gaze rakes over her body and I lean over her. "Don't move," I order, scraping my teeth over her shoulder, cupping her breasts and then dragging my hands down her ribcage, before I straighten and pull my shirt off. I stand there then, watching her, making her wait and I tell myself it's to drive the tension, to drive her to the edge, but another emotion claws at me, a need to control her, to control what she's become to me. What she can do to hurt me, like the rest of this fucking family, but she's not them.

Damn it.

I want to hate her.

I don't.

Not even close.

I undress, pull on a condom, and sit down on the couch and take her with me, pulling her onto my lap. Her hands come down on my shoulders. Our eyes lock, and holy hell, I feel this woman in ways I can't even describe. I lift her and press inside her. She takes me in a slow slide, and then she presses down, taking me all, straddling me.

Her teeth scrape her bottom lip and she moves back and forth, as if she just needs to feel me there, everywhere. I tangle my fingers into her hair and drag her mouth to mine. "Do you know what I want?" I demand.

"To hate me?"

"It would be easier that way."

"What would be?" she asks, breathlessly. "Fucking me?"

"Everything," I say. "Everything would be easier if I hated you like I do them, but no, I don't want to hate you. I don't want to forget you. Not anymore."

"Then what do you want?"

"Everything," I say, admitting out loud everything I feel with that one word. "Everything, Harper." I drag her mouth to mine and kiss her. She sinks into it, our mouths, our tongues, colliding with hunger, that's all I can call it—hunger. So damn much hunger, that we're touching each other, kissing each other, moving together, a sway of her hips, a pump of mine, repeat. There is nothing but us, here, now, and this. Whatever the hell this is, but I can't feel anything but her.

I pinch her nipple and she covers my hand on her breasts, kissing me even as we move. Everything. I want everything and more, I roll with her, pressing her back to the couch again and then I'm driving into her, pumping with a need that comes from somewhere deep, to the point that it's clawing. "Eric," she pants, and I kiss her, rolling to my side, and pulling her leg to my hip, thrusting as I do.

Her fingers dig into my shoulders and she pants my name again, and I thrust again. She buries her face in my chest and I can feel her quake before her body is spasming around me. God. I feel every moment of her orgasm, and it pulls me in, drags my release from me the way she pulls me to her and doesn't let go. My balls tighten, a knot of tension low in my groin, and then I'm shuddering into release with such intensity that I damn near black out.

When I come back to the world, I'm holding Harper, and she's holding me, our bodies molded intimately together, and I don't want to get up. I want to hold her, but there's a condom to consider. I pull back to look at her, and the minute our eyes connect, the pull between us is just as strong as before we fucked, and I know I'm here to stay. This isn't going to end like the other two times we were together. Because I'm not leaving. Not tonight. Not without her.

She's mine now. She's been mine since that night six years ago. It just wasn't our time yet, but now, now is our time and I'm not walking away. Not from the mess, the family dragged her into and not without her.

CHAPTER TWENTY-SEVEN

Eric

Still lying on the couch, still inside her, and still wearing the condom, I stroke a lock of hair from Harper's face. "I should get up."

"I know," she whispers and there's regret in her voice that stretches beyond this moment.

I cup her face and tilt her stare to mine. "I don't want to get up. I'm not leaving, Harper."

Her eyes soften, warm. "Good," she says. "I don't want you to leave."

"Good," I echo and kiss her. "But," I say seriously, "if I'm staying, you have to feed me. I'm wasting away here."

She laughs and it's a sexy, sweet laugh that I could easily find addictive. "We can't have that, now can we?" She shoves on my chest. "Get up and we'll eat."

I pull out of her and we both groan, with more laughter following. I help her to sit up and pull her to her feet. "I could hunt for the bathroom, naked but for a condom, or you could direct me to the right spot."

"I could enjoy the naked and wandering around my house option but since you're starving, there's one by the front door." She pushes to her toes and kisses me, the spontaneous act somehow as sexy as everything she just did when she was fucking me.

I pull her close and kiss her this time. "I'll be right back."

I scoop up my pants from the slate gray wood flooring, a color that matches the L-shaped couches that frame a stone fireplace, while the high back chairs by the window are a lighter gray. The décor is almost masculine until you add in

133

the fluffy cream colored throws and flower-shaped light bulbs dangling from above. This space is Harper. This is her space and I want to know her space. I want to know *her*.

I cross the room and the foyer to enter the bathroom, which is also all gray with white accents. Once I toss the condom into the trashcan, I pull my pants on commando style and lean on the sink, staring at myself in the mirror, and when I see my father in the image I look away; a thought I haven't had for years. A symptom of being here, I despise this place but I can't leave. I won't leave, not without Harper and I'm in this with eyes wide open and it doesn't seem to matter.

She's dangerous in ways she doesn't mean to be. She opens the door to this family, to the hate, on both sides. I've put her in the middle of that hate and she's put me in the middle of that hate. But it has to be this way because she needs out. I'm her way out.

I exit the bathroom and glance up the stairs where her bedroom must be located, where I plan to spend the night. Seeking her out, to tell her just that, I enter the living room to find her missing. "Harper?"

"I'm right here," she calls out, walking down the stairs, in a pair of black sweats and a pink T-shirt, her nipples that were just in my hands, puckering against the thin cloth. "I just couldn't put those work clothes back on."

I step to the bottom of the stairwell and when she reaches the last step, I wrap my arm around her and pull her to me. "I like you like this."

"Grunge princess?" she teases.

"Natural," I say. "I like you natural. Casual"

"Like you in your jeans and T-shirt at the office? That was a 'fuck you' to your father and brother, right?"

"I have no need to impress them," I say, "but *you* are another story."

"You impress me most naked," she teases.

"Is that right?"

"Yes. Definitely right." She takes my hand and starts walking backward. "I'm going to feed you now, but I have a condition."

134

"Another orgasm?"

She blushes a pretty pink that defies her comment about liking me naked. "Orgasms are always good," she says, releasing me as we enter the kitchen, "but I want you to tell me what all of your ink means."

"My ink," I repeat, when I'd expected her to want to know about my money, my success. Or even how I'm going to deal with Kingston. "That's what you want to know about me?"

"Yes," she says grabbing one of the takeout bags. "That's what I want to know about you. Because every choice you made to ink your body has to tell a story."

"It's the story of my life, sweetheart," I say, helping her unpack the food. "You're right about that."

"How old were you when you got your first tattoo?" she asks. "And before you answer, you're okay with me popping these in the microwave, right?"

"Of course," I answer, sitting down on a gray leather barstool. "And eighteen," I say, replying to her first question. I watch her pop one of the takeout containers in to warm. "It's a stopwatch that's still on my right forearm in the middle of more ink." I turn my arm and show her. "Pissed off my father which only made me like it more."

"And it means what to you."

"All things come in their own time. And that statement has meant many things to me in my life." My eyes meet Harper's. "Like us, sweetheart. It wasn't our time six years ago. It is now."

"All things come in their own time," she repeats softly, her gaze sliding over both of my arms. "You only had one sleeve when I met you six years ago."

"A lot has happened in six years."

"For you," she says. "I know it has."

"Not for you?"

"I feel like I've done nothing but fight the same battle." She gives a choked laugh. "You know that saying. The definition of stupid or insanity or whatever it is, is to keep doing the same thing and expecting a different result. You're right. Six years was too long." Pain stabs through her eyes but the microwave beeps and gives her an excuse to cut her stare. She looks away and pulls the first tray out, checking it and then replacing it with the second.

"This one is ready," she says, walking to set it in front of me.

I drag her to me, between my legs, not about to let her comments go unanswered. "You didn't make a mistake. There were times when I thought I left too soon and too easily."

"You didn't. You would never have been accepted."

"I know that," I say. "I knew that at the party. I didn't know it during some of those years in the SEALs."

"Yes, well as you said, six years makes me a damn slow learner."

"I never said that and it's clear that you stayed for your mother." The microwave goes off again. "How about some of that wine?" I ask. "It'll take the edge off."

"Yes," she agrees, "that would be good right about now."

"Where are the glasses?"

"Cabinet by the sink to the left."

I cup her head and kiss her and between the two of us, we sip wine and finish preparing the meal. This isn't a familiar thing for me. I don't do relationships. It's not what I want and yet, with Harper I enjoy this time with her and the very domestic act of preparing a meal together, even a warmed-up meal, is somehow more intimate than being naked on the couch earlier.

"It's chilly," she says when we've finished all of our prep. "I can turn on the fireplace in the living room if we eat in there."

A few minutes later we're settled on the floor in front of her coffee table eating. "My God, I missed this place," I say, the sauce and pasta coming together perfectly.

"It's really wonderful," she says. "I have a lot of favorite places around the area. North is one of the few places that has been here since you were here."

We sit and chat about the neighborhood until we're both done with our food. As we sit back and turn toward each other, she reaches out and catches my arm, tracing the rows of numbers randomly placed between a clock and a skull with an anchor.

"What do the numbers mean?"

"Numbers are how I process everything. If I'm thinking about anything, anything at all, there are numbers in my head."

"Even me?"

"Yes. Even you. It's a part of my life in all ways. It's how I make money. It's how I negotiate. It's how I brush my damn teeth. It's how I saw mission paths in the SEALs that no one else saw."

"SEAL Team Six," she says, running her finger over the skull and anchor before looking up at me again. "That's intense. You saw blood and death. I'm sure you had to take lives."

I cover her hand where it rests on my tattoo, and I don't even think about denying who I am. I was done with that a decade ago. "Is that a problem for you?"

"Of course not. You're a hero. I just hate that your family drove you to that life. You could have died. You have to have baggage from it."

"Less than you might think," I say. "I compartmentalize extremely well."

"I don't," she says. "I'm pretty all-in emotionally when I'm in. You should know that about me."

All in.

I *want* her all in.

I lean in closer, my hand on her cheek. "I want you all in."

Her hand covers mine on her face. "Until you leave again."

"Let me clarify what I just said. Yes, I shut people and things off easily, but not you. Never you."

"I didn't see you for six years, Eric."

"I told you. I thought of you often."

"As one of them."

"As the woman who wouldn't just fucking get out my head."

She pulls back. "Well, you wouldn't fucking get out of my head either."

"But you didn't come to me, did you?"

"You left in a way that made it clear you were done with me."

I lean back and hold out my right forearm, running a finger along a line of numbers with a crown at the end of it. "Do you know what that is?"

She sucks in a breath at the crown and covers it with her hand. "Is it bad? Is it something bad about me?"

"It says *Princess* in the numbers that correlate to the alphabet. I added it two full years after our night together."

"You tattooed the nickname you gave me on your body?"

"Yes, princess, *I did*. Now do you believe that I didn't forget about you?" I tangle my fingers into her hair and her hand settles on my chest. "Now isn't like the past. You know that, right? I didn't come here to walk away. Not from you."

"Eric," she whispers and I lean in to kiss her right as the doorbell rings, followed by pounding on the door. "Open up, Harper!"

At the sound of Isaac's voice, my jaw sets hard and Harper's eyes go wide. "This can't be good," she says, launching herself to her feet.

I'm standing with her by the time she's fully straightened. "Relax, sweetheart," I say, my hands settling on her arm, "He's a gnat that needs to be swiped. Nothing more. I'll handle my brother." I start to turn away and Harper grabs my arm.

"Wait," she says, pulling me around to face her. "Let me talk to him. Obviously my mother told him you're here. He's going to make a big deal out of this. I can shut it down."

I drag her to me. "You mean deny we're together?"

"No. That's not what I meant."

"Good. Because we're together now. That means we don't hide. And if that makes the Kingstons uncomfortable, fuck them. Do you have a problem with that?"

"No," she whispers. "You're right. Fuck them."

"Then I'll handle Isaac, sweetheart. No one has my brother's number like I do."

CHAPTER TWENTY-EIGHT

Eric

"Oh no," Harper says, catching my arm as I try to leave her to answer the door again. "I'm fine with Isaac knowing about us," she says when I turn back to her, "but you're shirtless and commando with your pants unzipped. That screams 'we're fucking' not 'we're together.' I draw the line there."

I cup her face and step into her. "Anyone in the same room with us for sixty seconds knows we're fucking, sweetheart."

"Don't taunt him with me. I don't like that. I don't want to feel like a weapon between two brothers, not even in a war I invited you into."

"I don't like how that sounds," I say, catching her hips and walking her to me. "What the hell does that mean?"

"Not now. Later. Right now, we have to deal with him so please, zip your pants and put on a shirt before you walk to the door."

I reach down and zip my pants before scooping up my shirt, my eyes never leaving her face. "You're going to explain whatever that was to me."

"I will," she promises. "I'll tell you."

"Yes, you will, princess."

Her eyes go wide and flare with anger that I don't stay to answer. Not when Isaac is shouting at the door again and pounding while holding a finger on the bell. "Jesus," I murmur, running a hand through my hair. "His degree of ridiculousness obviously hasn't changed." I take off for the door and this time Harper lets me go.

The ring and knock cycle has started again by the time I get there, along with another shout of, "I know you're in there, Harper! Damn it, open up."

I unlock the lock, open the door, and greet my brother, who's wearing a trench coat over the same three-piece suit he had on today that no doubt cost thousands. It also, from what I can tell, comes with a stick up his ass. "You're here for me, right?" I ask. "Here I am." I step forward, crowding him and forcing him onto the porch.

"I'm here for Harper," he says, unbuttoning his jacket and settling his hands on his hips.

After the exchange I just had with her, those words punch me in all the wrong ways. "To warn her away from me," I state, disliking the obvious history I don't know and Walker Security didn't tell me about in advance.

"Her mother is worried about her."

My lips quirk. "And you're the superhero here to pretend to save her while saving yourself? How'd that superhero routine work for you in the past?"

"There's nothing here for you."

"We both know that's not true. We both know that's never been true."

"You don't need the money. You want what no bastard deserves and you're using her and her ridiculous paranoia. She's your damn stepsister and you're fucking her, you sick fuck."

I smirk, unaffected by the ridiculous remark meant to get under my skin. He stopped getting under my skin about a year into this family. The problem for him is that's when I started getting under his skin. "Harper and I aren't blood," I say, "but we are, and we both know that's why she doesn't scare you, but I do." I step closer to him, damn near bringing us toe to toe. "And you should be afraid because we both know you're hiding something and we both know how good I am at finding out your secrets." It's a past that he can't run from, a past I don't want to run from. But then why wouldn't I? I'd fast-tracked to law school and joined him there. He'd hated it. He'd wanted an edge. He fucked our law professor to try to destroy me. He almost succeeded, but I one-upped him.

"I could have ended you."

"You should have done it while you could because that ship has sailed. Walk away, Eric. You don't know what pot you're stirring."

"But I want to and I will."

"I don't care about your fortune or the Bennett Empire behind you. Walk deeper into this and you might not walk away in one piece."

I arch a brow. "You're threatening me?"

"I don't need to threaten you. I'm stating a fact. Consider this a brotherly warning. The only one you'll receive. Get away from her before you take her down with you and all of us for that matter." He pokes a finger at my chest and that's one thing Isaac doesn't do. He doesn't get physical. "Go home now." He glares at me, but in the depth of his eyes, I see fear, the kind of fear I've seen in men's eyes seconds before they ended up dead. He turns and walks down the stairs, leaving every instinct I own saying this is bigger than I thought it was. Isaac is into something he can't get out of and it's time I meet with my father and find out if he's in it, too.

I walk to the railing to ensure Isaac leaves, a muscle in my jaw ticcing as I watch him shut himself inside his silver BMW. My grip tightens on the wood beneath my palms with a mental replay of his words: *I'm here for Harper. Get away from her before you take her down with you and all of us for that matter.* Isaac backs out of the driveway and I don't move until he's out of sight, my certainty that Harper is now ten feet deep in something that smells dirty and dangerous, absolute.

I turn back toward the house, an icy gust of wind rushing over me. It's nothing compared to the cold I've experienced in the past, during those years in the SEALs, and in too many ways, the year of my mother's death, ending in her suicide. Gigi had been the last one to see her, the last Kingston to taunt her. Nothing about that has ever felt right to me, which is exactly why Harper's alignment with Gigi will never be a comfortable one. I've accepted her reasoning, but her fucking

Isaac and then me in whatever order that I might have occurred, would not be.

I'm about to open the door, but at the same moment it flies open and Harper is standing there. "What happened?" she asks.

I advance on her, shut the door and lock it and then turn her to press her against it. "Did you fuck him?"

"No," she says. "I didn't fuck him. He tried. I turned him down. He's treated me like shit ever since."

"Then why protect him?"

"*Protect him*?" she asks, her tone incredulous. "I didn't protect him. I protected me and you. He's vicious. He lashes out. He competes with you and I'm not interested in being a pawn. And come on, Eric, you didn't want me to be a pawn to Gigi. But you're okay with using us to taunt him?"

"If he's uneasy, he makes mistakes. I'll catch him making those mistakes. I'll get you out of this."

"It's more than that and you know it. You want to hurt this family."

"Yes. I do. And I could have a thousand times over. Wanting and doing are two different things."

"Why didn't you?"

I look skyward, that question one I've asked myself over and over and come back to one place. I look at her and go there now. "Because my mother didn't want that. She protected them when they destroyed her. It was in the letter she left me. Which is exactly why I eventually left for the SEALs. I could have ruined Isaac. I wanted to. The temptation was too great. I had to leave. Every time I'm here, I have to leave. That's why I don't come here, but I came for you." My eyes meet hers. "The idea of you fucking him and fucking me is not a good one."

"I told you—no, I was never with Isaac." Her hand settles on my chest, that small touch burning through my body, *she* burns through me. "I didn't fuck him. I never wanted to fuck him and he hates me for it. Like you hate me. *Princess.* Already I'm her again and I can't be her." She shoves on my chest and tries to move away. "Let go."

Let go.

I should. I could. I'd be smart to do just that, but that's not going to happen. I'm not letting her go. I'm not going to walk away, and that might end up being the worst thing that ever happened to this family.

I tangle fingers into her hair and stare down at her. "I don't hate you. I'm obsessed with you."

"You can still hate me and be obsessed with me."

I kiss her, my tongue licking and exploring, looking for lies that I don't find. There's just a moment of resistance, then her sweet, soft submission, her soft curves melting against mine, her desire moaning from her lips. I want her submission. I want her desire. I want more than I should when I know I'm headed down a deep, dark rabbit hole, but Isaac was wrong. I won't be the death of her, but she might be the death of him because she's why I'm staying. She's why my mother's letter can't save him this time.

CHAPTER TWENTY-NINE

Eric

Dirty. Filthy. Fucking.

That's what I tried to make it between me and the princess, but now, here, in her foyer kissing her, I admit that it was never that. She slid right under my skin and stayed there from the moment I saw her across that pool. I don't want to let her go, but she, apparently, doesn't have the same sentiments right about now.

She shoves against my chest, tearing her mouth from mine. "No. No. My version of together isn't hatred and obsession. It's not me being a princess to you."

"Sweetheart, I tattooed *Princess* on my body. I tattooed *you* on my body."

"You also tattooed a jaguar on your shoulder in spite of your father."

"That jaguar isn't about revenge. It's about the world being bigger than the Kingston name. It's about not putting limits on myself. Everything inked on my body is a piece of me, Harper. You became that. You affected me."

"*You walked away.*"

"Be glad I did. I might have wanted you then, Harper, but I wasn't the same man I am now. It wasn't our time. *Now* is our time."

"And yet you came at me like I'm fucking your brother."

"I had no right to tell you that you couldn't, but had you fucked us both—"

"Oh God," she says, trying to pull away, but my leg slides against her knee, my hand going to the wall by her head.

"What just happened?" I demand.

"You implied that I'm some sort of whore who wants to do two brothers."

"I did no such thing. I told you how I feel."

"I slept with you. You affected me. You have always affected me, Eric, even when I wanted you out of my head."

"What does that mean?"

"It doesn't matter," she says, her eyes blazing with anger. "Let me off the wall."

"Not until you tell me what that means."

"You made me feel dirty, and like a weapon."

"You brought me here," I say. "And I told you: I came for you, not them."

"I don't like being put in the middle of Kingston drama. It's consumed my entire life."

"I'm not a Kingston if that's what you're implying."

"Yes, you are. You *are* a Kingston," she says. "You are your father's son just as much as I am my father's daughter."

"I was born a Mitchell and I will die a Mitchell."

"What are we doing right now, Eric?"

"You tell me. You're the one who pulled me into this and now you're telling me to let go."

Her expression softens. "I don't want you to let go."

"That's what you said. Let go. Your words, not mine."

"Those comments about me and Isaac turned me back into the enemy. Maybe not in context, but I felt the distrust in you. I heard it in the nickname, and don't tell me it's inked on your skin and that makes it okay. We both know it represents a divide."

"A divide that's now what brought us together."

"Don't let him divide us."

"He's not dividing us," I say. "I'm not walking away this time. This time is different. You have to know that. You have to feel that. We're together now."

"I don't know what that means."

"You do know. I know you know."

My cellphone rings, and I glance down at the number to find Grayson calling. I hit decline and curse under my breath. "Look, sweetheart, we need to talk but I'm negotiating the purchase of an NFL team and I have a small stake in the deal.

Grayson is calling me and he knows I came here for you. He wouldn't be calling if there wasn't a problem."

"You're—wait—you're buying an NFL team?"

"Packaging the project, but yeah. It's a big deal for the Bennett Corporation and for me."

"Take the call. That's incredible. I want to know what happened with Isaac, but I can wait."

"I'm going to call Grayson while I go to the hotel and grab my bag to move over here with you, unless you have a problem with that."

"I'd have a problem if you were staying at the hotel. That is unless I was with you."

"Good," I say, walking into the living room to finish dressing. "I want you to lock up." I say when she joins me. "If Isaac comes back, call me and don't open the door." I pull on my leather jacket and walk to the front of the house where I check the locks. Harper's in the foyer when I turn around.

"Do you think he plans to come back?" she worries. "What haven't you told me?"

"He's running scared," I say taking her hand, "and when he's scared, he acts erratically." I lead her into the kitchen and to the back door. "I'll explain my brother's version of crazy when I get back." I kiss her. "Flip the locks behind me."

"Okay, but now you've made me nervous, so hurry back, please."

"I will. I'll be fast." I exit the kitchen and wait for her to shut the door, then listen for the lock to flip into place.

I walk to the car and climb inside, dialing Grayson as I sink into the leather seat. "What's happening?"

"Julius Monroe is trying to back out," he says, of a major player in the NFL deal. "He won't talk to anyone but you."

"Fuck. What's his problem?"

"A competing bidder made a sweeter deal for him," Grayson says.

"Who the fuck is the competing bidder?"

"You tell me," Grayson says. "I didn't know we'd opened up a bidding process."

I scrub my jaw. "I'll call him and call you back." I start to hang up and he stops me.

"What's happening there?"

"I'm pretty sure my brother just threatened to kill me and Harper," I say. "If that doesn't tell you how well this is going, I don't know what will."

"Isaac talks a lot of big words," he says, knowing him well from Harvard where he and I met. "Same ol' Isaac, or something more this time?"

"He's scared. *Really* scared. Harper was right. She's over her head because he's over his head, and about to take her down with him."

"Then bring her here," he says. "Get her out of there."

Harper, in New York, in my bed. That works for me. Me leaving and not knowing this is over, doesn't work for me or her either though. "I might send her to you and then join her later."

"Send her. Sooner than later if she's in danger."

"I'll let you know and I'm calling Julius now." I disconnect and leave Julius a message.

I back out of the driveway and I'm about to pull away when I catch sight of a car parked to the far right, next to the curb with a light flickering behind the shaded window. Unease radiates through me, the kind that used to set me off while in the deep, dark bowels of enemy territory. That threat, the idea that Harper might know more than she thinks she knows, that someone might think she'll lead me there, hits ten wrong places in my gut. I back up, place the car in park and walk back to the door where I knock.

"Harper, it's Eric."

She opens the door. "What are you doing?"

I pull her to me. "Come with me. I want you with me."

"Yes," she says softly. "I want me with you, too."

"Good," I say. "I want you to want to be with me." I lead her to the car, and that feeling of uneasiness I'd felt with the idea of leaving her behind is not gone. In fact, it's stronger. Someone is watching us.

CHAPTER THIRTY

Eric

Halfway to the car, Harper shivers, and I pull her close, under my arm and against my body. "I should grab a coat," she murmurs.

"I'll get it for you and lock up," I say, wanting her inside the car where I can get her the hell out of here. I click the locks and open the passenger door. Obviously eager to get out of the cold, she slides into the seat. I kneel beside her, my hand settling on her leg, and when she looks at me, when this woman looks at me—and I mean every damn time—I want her. I want her in a bad way. Naked, yes, but it's more than that, it's deeper than that and I'm not even resisting.

I hand her my key. "Turn on the engine and the heat. There's a seat warmer, too."

"I know," she says. "Because I'm a Jaguar expert."

I arch a brow. "Are you now?"

"Of course I am. They're the enemy and the competition."

"But I'm not, sweetheart. Remember that. Where's your coat?"

"Pretty sure it never made it out of the kitchen."

"Got it. Lock the car door."

"What? Why?"

"Lock it, sweetheart." I don't give her time to ask questions I'm not going to answer until I get some precautions in place. I stand up and shut her inside, waiting until she clicks the locks. Then and only then do I head toward the house, walk inside and retrieve my phone from my pocket to dial Blake. "I have thirty seconds," I say when he answers. "I don't want Harper to hear this conversation until I have time to explain myself."

"I'm listening."

I grab Harper's coat and her keys from the counter and then step back into the doorway to keep an eye on the car. "There's someone staking out Harper's house in a black sedan. This, after my brother threatened me and Harper."

"Gut feeling about who's watching her?"

I step outside and pull the door shut. "I would if I had a damn gun and could yank the asshole in the car out and make him tell me. Hell, I might do it anyway."

"You think it's your brother's hired hands?"

"Maybe," I say, securing the lock, "but the look in Isaac's eyes tonight tells me that he's running scared. Really fucking scared. He's in trouble, which means Harper is in the line of fire."

"Always," he says. "I'll get you a weapon. Where are you headed and what's your plan?"

"We're about to leave for my hotel to grab my things, which is only three blocks away," I say, walking toward the car with a slow pace meant to buy time to end this call.

"You're staying with her then?" he asks.

"Damn straight I am. I came here for her. I'm keeping her safe and close."

"I'll leave a weapon outside her place and text you the location. And that data you needed is in the electronic folder I set-up for you along with my analysis. Text or call me when you look at it." He disconnects.

I stop at the car door and unlock it before climbing inside the now-toasty interior. "We're all set now," I say, offering her the coat.

"Thank you," she says. "I guess I really didn't need this. The car is warm and we're stopping right at the hotel door."

"The wind is still cold," I say. "Really cold. Is there a storm blowing in?"

"There's a winter storm warning," she says. "I saw it on my phone earlier. And normally my mother would be the weather woman warning me."

"She sent Isaac to warn you instead," I say, shifting the car into reverse.

"You're the bastard storm?"

"That's not always a bad thing to be," I say, backing us up and then placing us in drive, easing us down the path and eyeing the car that's still parked in the same spot.

My cellphone rings and I grab it to find Julius returning my call. "I have to take this. There are problems with the NFL closing."

"Of course," she says. "Take it. Then you can tell me what you haven't told me. No secrets, right?"

No secrets.

I can't agree to that statement. I do have secrets. Secrets she won't like. Secrets I don't intend for her to find out. "We'll talk," I say instead and answer my call.

⸙

Harper

We'll talk.

Not "no secrets." I don't miss that sidestep and if he thinks I will, he's forgotten that I've survived the Kingstons for six long years. He, who is all about me not keeping anything from him, says "we'll talk" to my request for no secrets. I don't know what that means, but I don't like it.

"No," he says, to whoever he's talking to. "That's not the deal." He's calm but hard, a sharp-edged quality to his seemingly nonchalant tone that I'm not sure is about me or his caller. "I don't like being played with," he adds. "We'll replace you." He disconnects the call and we pull up to the hotel and the valets are immediately upon us.

I slip on my coat even as I step outside. I round the vehicle as Eric palms the driver a large bill, a hundred, I think, which drives home his success, but more so, it shows a generous side of this self-made man. Someone I don't believe has lost touch with where he came from, or he wouldn't be so eager to dress down his success. Perhaps only his secrets. This idea sets me on edge again and I have to rein myself back in. Do I really want to go down this "no secrets" path? Do I really want to open that door? Haven't I already? There are parts of me I don't know if I can ever expose. Mistakes I've made. Things I know that would hurt him. I don't want to hurt this man. I'm falling in love with him, and that very idea has me walking into the hotel rather than waiting on him, afraid he'll see. Afraid I'll scare him away and he won't want to stay and help.

I push through the automatic revolving doors and suddenly Eric is behind me, taking the small moving space with me, his body pressed to mine, his hands on my waist. His mouth at my ear as he says, "You don't mind if I join you, do you?"

"Depends," I say and then I don't know what I'm doing. I push the buttons I don't want pushed back. "Are you going to tell me your secrets?" We clear the doors at that moment and he doesn't reply. He simply pulls me under his arm and aligns our hips, casting the staff to our left and right random greetings before we cut left past the security desk and reach the elevator bank with two cars.

He punches the button and one of them opens, his fingers lacing with mine as he guides me inside and uses his card to key in his floor. The minute the doors shut, he pulls me to him, his fingers tangling in my hair, his thick erection throbbing against my belly. "My secrets would hurt you more than they'd help us." And then he's kissing me, drugging me with the rich, spicy taste of his tongue on my tongue, driving away my need to know what he means. Because there is more in this kiss, too. There is the taste of certain pain. He will hurt me. He will leave me. And this time he'll take everything I am when he does, and I can't even seem to care.

CHAPTER THIRTY-ONE

Harper

"Damn coats," Eric murmurs, trying to pull me closer, but settling for another kiss, his tongue licking into my mouth for a deep stroke that I feel from head to toe, inside and out. I always feel this man inside and out. I have always felt this man in a complete, consuming way, even when we were apart, even when I was with other men. And the way he's kissing me, the way he seems to drink me in, leaves nothing behind. He takes all there is to take. He takes all of me and I can't stop it from happening. I can't protect myself with Eric.

He's danger.

He's safety.

The elevator dings and he reluctantly parts our lips, his hand stroking my hair in an act that is somehow tender and erotic at the same time. "Let's go to the room," he says, his voice low, gravelly. Affected. I affect this gorgeous, intense, brilliant man, and even now, I have moments like this one where that doesn't feel possible. I'm the enemy. I'm the princess. I'm hated and I've even felt that in his touch, in his kiss, only I don't feel that hate anymore.

"Yes," I say softly. "Let's go to the room," I add.

His eyes smolder with amber heat in reply, with none of the ice I've seen there on random occasions to be found. I hate that ice. I love the fire, banked just behind those embers. He laces the fingers of one of my hands with the fingers of his and leads me toward the hallway. We cut right and I'm relieved and surprised to find his room a short walk to our immediate left. We stop at his door and nerves flutter in my belly as if I haven't spent hours with him this very night, as if this right now will be our first time together. He doesn't give me time to live inside those nerves though. He pulls me in front of him, his big body behind mine, and even with my coat on I am aware of every inch of hard muscle pressing against me, promising wicked dirty deeds to follow.

He opens the door, and when I would dart into the room, he holds onto me, keeps me with him, and walks me forward while he stays at my back. The door slams shut, and I think he locks it, but I can't be sure. He eases us forward into the room and then shifts behind me. His jacket lands on a desk in the living room to my right. Already he's dragging mine off my shoulders, but even as he does, he keeps me in front of him, holding onto me as he drops my coat on top of his.

Then his hands are sliding up my stomach, under my T-shirt, dragging it over my head. It's barely hit the floor when his hands are on my breasts and he's leaning forward, his lips at my ear. "Do you feel me the way I feel you, Harper?" he asks, his breath a warm fan on my neck that still manages to shiver down my spine. His lips are a whisper of a touch like his words at my ear.

"You know I do," I say, my voice raspy, affected, my hands covering his hands.

"Are you sure about that?"

"Let me turn around and ask me again when you're looking at me."

"I'm not ready for you to turn around," he says, tilting my head back and bringing our lips together. "I was never ready for you." I'd insist the opposite was true, but he doesn't give me the chance. "What am I feeling, Harper?"

"Tell me," I say, wishing he'd let me turn around, some part of me wondering if I'm facing forward because he's feeling exactly what I felt downstairs: vulnerable inside my own emotions.

"*What am I feeling, Harper*?" he presses.

I say what I feel. "Resistant."

He goes still, utterly still, and then he's turning me to face him, his hands shackling my waist. "Resistant to what?"

"Me. Us. This."

He tangles his fingers in my hair and kisses me, a wicked thrust of his tongue against my tongue before he demands, "Does that taste like resistance?"

"It tastes like you claiming control, like you need it."

His hand slides under my sweats and he squeezes my bare backside. "I seem to remember you liking me in control."

"I do," I dare. "I like it a lot when I shouldn't."

"Why shouldn't you, Harper?"

"It's not what I do. I don't let other people take control. That's not what my father taught me, but this family, the Kingston family, takes and takes that from me."

"I'm not a Kingston."

He's right. For the first time since he's denied that birthright, I let him. I understand now that it's not about what he deserves. It's about who he is, who he's become. Where he came from. My hand flattens on his chest. "No. You're a Mitchell and I like that about you."

He stares down at me, shadows in his eyes, a storm in their depths before he's kissing me again and it's wild, taut with emotion, demanding. He's demanding, and when I've just lost myself to the passion, his mouth is gone, and he's turning me to face the other way again. It's the control thing once more. He needs it. He has to have it. It runs deeper than us. It's about who he is at his core, who life has made him. And I like it. I do. It's like I need to let him have control. Like I need things I didn't know I needed and it's all about him.

He leans in and I feel him pull off his shirt before he's pressing his naked torso against me, reaching forward to grip my thighs before dragging his hands upward over my hips to cup my breasts again, his teeth scraping my shoulder before he whispers, "You do have control, Harper. All of the control and I *don't* let anyone else have control." He kneels and drags my pants down my legs. His teeth scraping my hip now, but he doesn't stay on his knees, he doesn't leave me where I'm at as I expect.

He rotates me and suddenly he's kissing me and my palms are pressed to warm, taut skin over rippled, perfect muscle. The man is hard all over and I need that hardness next to me, inside me. "Eric," I whisper, sliding my hands under his waistband. "I need—"

"Me too, sweetheart," he says, kissing me again, and then he's releasing me long enough to grab his wallet and hand me a condom. "I'll put you in charge of this," he says, heat radiating between us, but the condom hits a hotspot in my chest that I don't like.

He undresses, and all that perfection is now exposed, his cock jutting forward, his ink on display in all its glorious, colored perfection, but still, the condom burns a hole in my hand. Eric's hands come down on my shoulders and he drags me to him. "What just happened?"

What just happened?
There's the question.
The one I now have to answer.

CHAPTER THIRTY-TWO

Harper

Eric cups my face, forcing my gaze to his, while his cock is thick at my hip, all that hard perfection of his tall, muscular body pressed next to me. "What just happened?" he repeats.

"Can you just kiss me again already?" I ask, his heart thundering beneath my palm, or maybe it's mine radiating down my arm. I don't know.

"Talk to me, Harper," he prods softly and I know he's not going to let this go. I want him to let this go. I need to get out of my own head right now.

"This is what happened," I say, pushing to my toes and pressing my lips to his at the same moment that I wrap my hand around his cock.

One of his hands cups my head, the other gripping my backside as he gives me what I want. He kisses the hell out of me, drugging me with the taste of him, and driving away anything but him and now. He maneuvers us and sits down on the couch, pulling me onto his lap, his erection in between us and a condom burning a hole in my palm. I will not think about the past. I will not think about my secret.

I open the package and roll it down the hard length of him and by the time I'm done, he's already kissing me again, molding me close; my breasts to his chest.

"Harper," he says roughly against my lips and then he's tangling his fingers in my hair, using an erotic tug to force my gaze to his. "I'm no virgin, sweetheart. I'm no angel and I've had my share of fucks, but the condoms are all about you and me and us. I bought them for us."

"I didn't ask," I say, wishing that was all that was on my mind but still appreciating what he's trying to do. The way he wants me to see just me and him.

"You wanted to ask," he says. "You should have. I told you. We're together now." He seals those words with a kiss and then lifts me, pressing inside me, stretching me, and then I'm sliding down the hard length of him. My hands go to his shoulders and our eyes lock, my sex clenching around him with the impact of this connected moment.

His eyes rake over my pebbled nipples and lift to my face, lingering on my mouth and lifting to my eyes. "You're beautiful," he says, his tone somehow sandpaper and silk on my nerves. I'm affected by how he looks at me, by how he touches me. By how he murmurs, "Come here," and tangles his fingers in my hair again, dragging my mouth to his. "I don't want to fuck anyone else but you. I don't want you to fuck anyone else but me."

It's everything I want and yet it's terrifying. I'm going down the rabbit hole where there will be no return, to a place where my secrets matter, to a place where his might as well. "I don't want anyone else but—"

"No buts about this," he says. "I'm not sharing you." His voice is low, guttural in a way that says he means what he's saying. In a way that says he's one hundred percent invested in me. And with that, with his intensity, he undoes me. "I want things from you that I shouldn't want."

"Why?" I ask and I forget my secrets, my elbow softening with the need to keep him close when he seems to be trying to convince himself he should push me away. "Why shouldn't you want them? The princess thing again?"

"You mistake the meaning behind that name. You don't understand what it means to me." He doesn't give me time to ask, to demand an explanation to something I feel has been almost a weapon between us. His mouth is on my mouth, his tongue thrusting past my lips, and then doing a deep slide that has me moaning into his mouth, and digging my fingers into his shoulders.

He responds to my response, deepening the kiss, and running his hands up and down my back, his touch electric, a charge that dances along my nerve endings and heats every part of me. Everything but this man and the sensations he creates in me fades away. There is just us moving, us swaying, us kissing and every touch is one part erotic, and one part tender—a pinch of my nipple, the caress of his lips. The hard drive of his cock, the gentle stroke of his tongue. The smack of my backside and then his cheek to my cheek, followed by a squeeze as he whispers, "I should be walking away, but I can't. You won't let me."

"What does that mean? I won't let you? Do you want me to let you go?"

He rotates me as he had earlier and presses my back to the couch. "No," he shocks me by saying. "I don't. I'm in this now. I'm not walking away. It's you who will walk away."

"Are you telling me you're going to make me hate you, Eric? Are you telling me there's something I don't know?"

"I'm telling you that you won't like all that you'll find out about me. You should walk away because I won't. You should, *but don't.*" His mouth slants over mine and then he's kissing me, driving into me, and I can feel him trying to hold onto control, but there is an edge to him, a need that radiates through me and with every thrust and grind. I arch into him, I meet his need and I know the moment he loses that control. The moment he tastes and feels nearly desperate and it feeds that in me. I *am* desperate, for more of him, all of him, even that part of him he doesn't want me to see or know. I don't know in this space and time where I end and he begins. I only know need and passion and then finally the intense wave that comes over my body and blooms into the quake of my body, into release. Eric follows with a guttural groan and a shuddering of his body.

When our bodies calm, and he's rolling us to our sides again, I become aware of his cellphone ringing. "Your phone," I murmur, a remote memory coming to me. "I think it was buzzing the entire time we were busy."

"*Busy?*" he laughs. "Yes, we were busy."

My cheeks flush and he pulls us both to a sitting position before brushing his lips over mine. "Let's get out of here. Until I can get you in my bed, I want to be in yours."

His bed?

I'm not sure what to do with that, considering his bed is in New York City, and yes I can visit him, but then what?

"I won't leave my mom behind. You need to know that."

He walks to a trashcan, sheds the condom and then reaches for his pants, pulling his phone out from inside, reading a message before he pulls on his pants. "We'll talk about it."

"No," I say standing up, that comment reading like another play for control. "We won't." I grab my tee and pull it on and as I reach for my pants he pulls me around to face him.

"We'll make sure your mother's safe," he says. "We'll protect her. I promise you." He cups my face. "*I promise.* Don't close the door on us."

I open my mouth to respond when the word *safe* takes me off guard. "*Safe.*" I say. "Not—we'll protect her from legal issues, but safe. What does that mean? Is she in danger?"

His jaw sets hard. "Let's get dressed and talk."

My heart starts to race. "Eric, damn it, is she in danger?"

"Put on your clothes, Harper."

He releases me and grabs my pants. "Get dressed." He turns away and grabs his T-shirt, pulling it over his head. I decide I need to be dressed, too, just like he said. Dressed equals control and right now, I feel like I have none. We sit down side by side to lace our shoes and his phone buzzes with another message that he replies to, his jaw setting hard before he sticks his cell in his pocket. I stand up and face him, my arms folding in front of me.

"Talk."

He stands, towering over me, as his hands come down on my shoulders. "I'm working with a top-notch security company to find answers. Walker Security sports a staff that includes ex-special forces, CIA, and FBI, and the list of skills and backgrounds are long. Their skills along with mine will uncover what's happening with Kingston Motors."

"That's not what you want to say right now," I say, aware he hasn't told me everything. I sense it. I can almost taste it in the air.

"I had Blake, my contact at Walker, get someone from his team in place at your house."

His push for locked doors comes back to me hard and fast. "Why? Just say it."

"Someone's watching your house, which most likely is nothing more than my brother's paranoia over my presence and a private eye that he's hired to keep an eye on me or us."

"Most likely? What are the other options?"

His fingers flex on my shoulders. "Whoever this is either wanted me to see him, or he's really bad at his job. Either way, I'm going to talk to him."

"Talk to him? Are you crazy? What if he has a gun?"

"I'm not without skills, sweetheart. That part of my life you missed, and I'm glad you did." There's a knock on the door. "Blake sent one of his men over to stay with you."

"Stay with me? I'm not staying here. This is crazy and if you're going to be crazy, I'm going with you."

"I swear to God, Harper, I will tie you to the bed and keep you here. Stay here. It will take half an hour at most."

"Do not go caveman on me," I warn.

"You wanted my help. You wanted *me*."

"I do want you, alive and well."

"I'm right here, Harper, and I protect what matters to me. I'll protect *you*. Don't fight me on this. I need to talk to this guy before he's gone."

I matter to him. That brings me down about ten notches. I inhale and let my breath out. "Yes. Okay."

"Blake's man is going to stay at the door to be sure you're safe. Come lock up."

He leads me to the door and when he would leave, I catch his arm. "Please don't get hurt."

He cups my head and kisses me. "I'll be right back." He releases me and exits the room. I lock the door and lean against it, all too aware of the obvious. If Eric didn't think there was a real threat, there wouldn't be a guard at my door. He also didn't promise not to get hurt.

CHAPTER THIRTY-THREE

Eric

I exit the hotel room to be greeted by a burly guy with a beard wearing a blue suit and an earpiece. He gives me a nod. "I'm Jensen," he says.

I don't introduce myself. He knows who I am. I'm also not letting any guy I don't know into a room alone with my woman, even Blake's guy, any more than I'm going to leave her exposed to danger. If this turns out to be trouble, I'm getting her the hell out of here. "Don't let anyone in or out of that room."

"Understood. Adam's in town. He's at the house."

Adam being an ex-SEAL, who I didn't serve with but I know and respect, from Blake's operation back in New York City. I give a nod and add, "I'll be back in half an hour."

I don't say more. He understands. If I'm longer, there's a problem. I head down the hallway with the scent of Harper on my skin and the taste of her on my lips, the idea that I almost left her to deal with this alone, not a good one. She needed me. I needed to be here. I needed to be here a long damn time ago and maybe she wouldn't still be here in this mess. She's not staying and I'm not leaving without her.

Eager to deal with this problem and get back to her, I reach the end of the hallway and don't bother with the elevator. I take the stairs and I'm at the front of the hotel, but I don't stop for my car. I walk toward Harper's house and dial Blake. "Talk to me."

"He's still there," he says. "And the plates are registered to one of the neighbors."

"He pulled them off another car."

163

"That's my bet."

"That's not a stupid, half-assed, PI move," I say.

"Not all PI's are stupid," he counters. "Quite the contrary." He moves on. "Glock at the back door in the bush. I only had two men available and one is tracking down Isaac. Adam's with you. He'll find you when you need him."

"Got it." I disconnect as my eyes find the car still parked in the same spot, but I don't give the driver time to see me.

I cut left down the side of one of the neighbor's houses without any resistance. I enter the unfenced backyard and cross two more open rear yards before I'm moving through the shadows of Harper's property and arrive at her back door. I grab the Glock and holding a weapon, any weapon, is like holding an old friend in my hand. Automatically, my training kicks in, I check the ammunition, and shove the weapon into my waistband, under my jacket before I head to the side of the house.

Once I'm there, I find the car still boldly parked across the street, almost daring me to confront him. I rest my back against the wall and Adam, dressed in all black, down to the beanie on his otherwise curly black hair, appears by my side. "He's alone," he says. "I think he wants to talk. You don't announce yourself to a SEAL and expect to be ignored."

A SEAL.

Not ex-SEAL.

Because a SEAL is always a SEAL and we both get that.

"Agreed," I say, "and if he wants to talk, I'm not going to disappoint him."

"I do like how you think." He pulls his weapon. "I'll cover you."

I push off the wall and start walking toward the front of the house. The minute I clear the wall and the bushes, that brings me into the open, the driver revs the engine of his car, rolls down the window and holds up a lit cigarette. He starts rolling forward and tosses it, along with something else. He floors it then and drives away. I walk toward the cigarette and stop next to it, but I'm more interested in the rolled-up piece of paper next to it. Adam pulls a pair of rubber gloves from his pocket and hands them to me.

I pull them on and squat down to grab the rolled-up paper and find a line of numbers with random letters. My brain plays with them—translating letters to numbers and the reverse—memorizing the fourteen digits before I toss the paper and the cigarette into the baggy Adam is holding open for me. "What was it?" he asks, eyeing the items in the bag. "A code? Aren't you a numbers guru?"

"It's not a cipher, code, or a translatable message. It's not even a point in history. It's an identifying number, like a name, but it's not a VIN number or even a parts number."

He gives me a deadpan look. "You know all of that in the sixty seconds you were looking at that number?"

"Yes," I say. "And as you said, he wanted to talk and that's what he did." I motion to the bag. "That's a message. If we find out what the identifier's attached to, we'll understand that message."

"Or it's a distraction to focus you in the wrong direction," Adam says as we walk to the front of the house.

His pocket vibrates and he pulls his phone out and glances at a message while I consider his thoughts. It could be a distraction, but if it is, it's someone who's studied me. Someone who knows how damn obsessed I can get about a series of numbers. Isaac isn't that detailed or focused. My father is another story. He knows the savant in me once struggled to spread my focus, but thanks to special training in the Navy, I'm beyond that.

"Isaac's at his home," Adam says, sliding his phone back into place. "He went straight there from here. He didn't meet with anyone."

"Anyone but you watching his house?"

"No one. You think he's being targeted, too? I thought you believed he was behind this tonight?"

"I'm not ruling out anything right now. Isaac is running from more than me and Harper. Was tonight related to his fear? Yes, but I'm not sure how. Was tonight's visitor a tipster trying to help? A hired goon trying to fuck with my head? Someone trying to mock me with the message in numbers? The options are many."

"Agreed. We're in this to end it with you. I'm here. The job I came for is over. I'm not going back to New York until you go back. You staying here or at the hotel?" he asks.

"Here," I say, disliking hotels where strangers come and go too easily.

"Then so am I." He motions toward the side of the house and then heads that way and I don't even care that anyone watching knows he's here. In fact, I'm glad they know to stay the hell away.

I scan the area but I see no one and feel no one. I start walking and reach in my pocket, removing a mini Rubik's cube, and while I once had to actually work the puzzle to focus my mind, I now just need to hold it to mentally work the challenge of it and whatever I'm trying to focus on outside of it. My mind chases those numbers, looking for their meaning: an employee badge number, a reference number to a medical claim. The list becomes a dozen long by the time I reach the hotel and Blake is calling me.

"The numbers mean nothing to you, genius?" he asks, as I enter the lobby and head toward the stairs. "What the fuck?"

"They're an identifier," I say, moving my weapon the rear of my pants. "In other words, Mr. Hacker Genius. Find out what they identify."

"Already working on it. It's not a VIN number or car part."

"I already told Adam that. Think outside of the box. I'll send you a list of prospects if you need them, but of course, you're a genius hacker, right?"

"You just can't stand the idea of someone else being the genius, now can you?"

"I'll believe you're a genius when you find out what that identifier means."

"Rolling my sleeves up now, asshole. Get ready to feel stupid for once. And while I'm the genius hacking, our lab will run prints of the stuff you and Adam bagged tonight. How present do you want my men in Denver?"

"Present, but out of sight until we know what the hell really happened tonight."

"What's your gut?"

"That this is a symptom of a bigger problem and we don't know the real problem or who is behind that problem."

"Agreed," Blake says.

We talk another minute, and disconnect right as I exit to my floor, my hand back on the Rubik's cube. By the time I reach my door and relieve Jensen of his duties, I've decided to look to the obvious place for an answer to what that identifier represents—Harper. That man was at her house. It hits me then; I've been assuming the message is for me because of the numbers when it could be for her. Certainty fills me; the message is for Harper and for reasons that are pure instinct, that feels like a problem. That feels dangerous. It feels like something else Harper still hasn't told me and if she was anyone else, I'd have already homed in on there being more to know with her.

I've said it, and now I feel it ten-fold: I can't trust my instincts with this woman. I'm too fucking insanely into her. And the very idea that at this point, Harper could be holding information back, does not sit well. I want answers or I'm out.

I slide my keycard into the room door and open it. I've made it all of four steps when Harper charges at me, flings herself into my arms, and breathes out, "Thank God."

Thank God, spoken with relief.

"I was so worried." She pulls back to look at me. "I'm glad you're back."

She has a million questions, I'm certain, but she's not asking them. She's focused on me and I don't remember the last time anyone worried about me or focused on me for any reason that wasn't to hurt me or compete with me. I don't remember a time when anyone defended me as she did with her mother. Her mother, who is all she has, the only one she calls family. No one understands that more than me. With that thought, I decide right now that if she's hiding something, she's afraid. Words Grayson has said to me over and over come back to me: *You get what you give.* If I don't give Harper my trust, she will never give me hers. She doesn't trust me with her secret because she doesn't trust me not to leave. I've done so two times before. I earned her distrust.

I tangle my fingers into her hair and kiss her. "I'm not going anywhere. Watch and see."

Her eyes cloud and darken. "Promise?"

"Yes, Harper, I promise. Now, take me home to your bed."

"Is it safe?"

"Yes. I'll tell you everything on the way. Just like I hope you will tell me everything. When you're ready."

I don't give her time to deny or reply. I don't place that pressure on her. I kiss her again, grab my bag, and lead her to the door. I'm giving her my trust. I'll earn hers. And I won't allow either of us to regret those decisions.

CHAPTER THIRTY-FOUR

Eric

I manage to usher Harper to the elevator without much explanation, but once the car doors shut and I've punched in the lobby level, she's ready for answers. "What happened when you went to my house and why do you want to get back there now with such urgency?"

Because I want her back home where I know we're secure, where I can control our environment, and Walker Security is guarding the exterior or the property. "That was the whole idea," I say instead. "Get my bag. Go back to your place."

Her lips purse. "We're in this together, remember? No secrets, Eric. I deserve to know what just happened at my own home. Why did you rush me here only to rush me back?"

"I don't like group settings with unknown elements at play."

"Meaning the guy watching my house," she assumes.

"The entire situation doesn't feel right. You were right to pull me into this."

"I hated pulling you in."

"I don't," I say and intend to move on to the message we received tonight, eager to find out if she knows what it means, but she gets there first.

"The car at my house, Eric. Tell me what happened."

"The minute I walked in his direction, he rolled down the window and tossed a cigarette and note out."

"A note? What kind of note?"

"A piece of paper with a fourteen-digit sequence of numbers and letters."

She frowns. "Nothing but the sequence? That's odd."

"Correct," I say.

"Then it has to be a message for you, right? Your genius doesn't scare whoever is behind it. Or they know you. They know how you operate."

"Or it's meant for you," I say.

"Me?" Her brow furrows. "Maybe," she says, showing no resistance to the idea. "It was my house he was watching, but the numbers feel related to you, not me. Do you understand what they mean?" The elevator dings and the doors open.

We step into the lobby and start walking toward the door. "It's a name that isn't a name," I say, and when most people would just stare at me after a statement like that, she follows my lead immediately.

"Like a VIN or part number?" she asks.

"It's neither of those things. I'm hoping once you look at it it'll mean something to you." We exit the front of the hotel and I pull my phone from my pocket and key in a message. "I just sent you a text with the sequence," I say, following her to the car door that the doorman is holding open for her. "See what it means to you, if anything."

"I left my phone at home."

I hand her mine with the message pulled up, and palm the doorman a large bill, as he helps her into my rental. Once I join Harper in the car, I place us in drive and glance her direction. "Any idea what it means?"

"I wish I did," she says, "But I don't." She turns my direction, engaged, not avoiding. My paranoia over the message being for her was about my need to protect myself when I'm supposed to be protecting her. "You're sure it's not a parts number?" she asks.

"I'm one-hundred-percent positive," I say. "It's not a parts number, or not one in any recognized database."

"But there's so many parts and manufacturers and—"

"It's not a parts number," I say, turning us toward her house.

"What about a VIN number for a competitor?"

"No."

"How do you know?" she presses. "I mean, I get that you're a numbers guy, but VIN numbers could be data added and deleted from databases that you might not have access to."

"It wouldn't be sequenced in that manner," I insist, pulling us into her driveway. "But we're not without resources. Blake Walker is considered one of the best hackers in the world. He'll look for a connection that isn't obvious."

"The part where he's a hacker. Is that a good or bad thing?"

"He's one of the good guys. The kind our own military contacts for help. He's going to run the sequence and see what technology reveals." I park and kill the engine.

"Okay, then another question: is this a warning or a clue?"

"If it were a warning, it would be something more obvious."

"Right," I say. "I mean, people have died. It makes sense someone would want to help us. People closer to this than I am in some way. It makes sense they'd know you to be the one that would stand up against the Kingstons." Her gaze goes to her door. "I bought this place a year after meeting you, my escape from Kingston hell." She glances over at me. "I didn't know you'd lived in this area and yet I gravitated here. That's odd, right?"

"Kismet, sweetheart," I say softly.

"Yes," she says, the air thickening between us. "Kismet."

I stroke her cheek. "Let's go inside." I reach for the door.

She grabs my arm and her attention is riveted on the house. "Are you really sure this is a good idea? Is it safe?"

"You have me, sweetheart," I say giving her a wink. "You're safe."

"From everyone *but* you?"

I lean over and stroke her cheek. "If you had protection from me, how would I ravish you night and day?"

She laughs and strokes her fingers over my jaw. "And I do want to be ravished by you."

"That's what I want to hear." I kiss her and straighten. "I'll grab my bag and then come around and get you. Wait on me."

I exit the car, waste no time grabbing my bag, and right as I reach the passenger door, Harper pops it open. I offer her my hand and pull her to her feet and to me. Her arms wrap my waist, and I know the moment her hand manages to hit the gun she's miraculously missed until now. Her eyes rocket to mine. "Walker armed me," I explain.

"Right. Well, Mr. Navy SEAL. I'm not complaining. I approve and so would my father. He made me learn to shoot, and I carry."

"Do you now?"

"Yes. I do. I should never have left without my purse or my Baby Glock."

It's not the weapon I'd choose for her, but we'll deal with that another time. She's carrying, and that could be a good thing or a bad thing. Weapons can be used against you if you don't handle them correctly. "How often do you practice using it?"

"Not as often as I should."

I take her hand and start walking toward the house. "We'll fix that," I say, digging her keys from my pocket to quickly turn the locks and shove open the door. "Your castle awaits."

She shivers and snuggles deeper into her coat, but she just stares at the door, nervous to enter her own safe place. I pull her in front of me, my body cradling hers. "You have me, remember? You're safe, and as a bonus, Walker has a man watching the house." I nuzzle her ear. "I got you, Harper, and one day you'll know that."

She darts away with those words, grabs her phone from the island, and then turns to face me. "Don't make promises you can't keep."

I shut the door and lock it before giving her my full attention. "I never make a promise I can't keep."

"Actually, I said don't make promises, but I don't think you've really made any. I don't know what I'm talking about. My room is upstairs." She turns away and starts walking.

I don't stop her. I follow. Her room and her bed seem like the perfect place to finish this conversation.

CHAPTER THIRTY-FIVE

Eric

I follow Harper up the stairs, and I don't waste any time doing it. The last thing I want is for her to find more reasons to divide us and that's what she just tried to do; divide us, pull back. *Push* back. I grab my bag and I'm behind her by the time she's halfway up the stairs. With a few skipped steps, I'm at the door to her bedroom moments after she enters.

I pause in the doorway as she takes off her coat and tosses it onto one of two large gray chairs in front of a garden window, and I take in a room as masculine as her living room. The bed is king-sized with a slate gray headboard that matches the chairs. The floor is also gray. The only thing feminine about the space is Harper herself and the red pillows and red lampshades. Even the lamps are gray. Her décor now strikes me as a window into who she's become. She's living in a Kingston, male-dominated world, barely holding onto herself. I'm going to change that.

She steps to the side of the bed and sets her phone on the nightstand as if she just needs something to do with herself. I toss my bag on the chair next to her coat, remove my gun and stick it inside the bag, and then drop my own coat next to hers. We stand there, staring at each other, intimacy weaving between us. "I am glad you're here. That's all. I just want you to know that whatever else happens, I'm glad you're here." She cuts her gaze and tries to turn away.

I catch her arm and turn her to me. "Me, too, Harper. Me fucking, too. Why don't you understand that? I didn't come to help you. I came because I couldn't fucking turn away. If I had my way, I'd take you and your mother the hell out of here, and we'd leave Isaac to burn in hell on his own."

"She won't leave. She won't, Eric."

"Get her to," I say. "Convince her staying is dangerous."

"Is it?"

"Dangerous enough to get your mother out of here and for me to get you out of here."

"I can't leave. I could have access to information we need."

"Blake has everything you could have and more at his fingertips."

"There's value to in-person, physical presence to investigate, especially when my mom's on the line."

"She's not a strong person," I say. "You are. Get her out," I repeat.

"How? How do I do that? I have nothing but my suspicions to support her leaving, and that's not enough. She's afraid to be without your father."

"But does she love him?"

"No. I don't think so. No. I know she doesn't. She doesn't act at all with him like she did with my father."

"Then she'll leave him. Let's find the motivation for her to get out." I grab my briefcase and set it on the bed. "Let's dig in."

"My briefcase is still in the car," she says. "I need to grab it." She glances at the door and I don't miss her unease. I'm driving home the theme of danger. It's messing with her head.

"I'll grab it. You get comfortable." I head that direction and as I walk down the stairs, my phone buzzes with a text from Blake that reads: *I hacked the HR files and looked at employee numbers and even union membership numbers for Kingston. No go. No matches. Still working. More when I know something.*

I shove my phone back into my pocket and go grab Harper's briefcase. Once I'm back upstairs in the bedroom, I find Harper barefoot on the bed, and it doesn't matter that she's in sweats and a tee. My cock throbs. I want to strip her naked. I want to fuck her. I want to make love to her. But I need her out of this Godforsaken city.

I cross to the bed and set her briefcase down. "Thank you," she says, giving me this sweet, sexy look that almost changes my priorities to dirty play instead of my dirty brother.

I sit down next to Harper and we both unpack our computers. For me, that means my MacBook and a full-sized Rubik's cube. Harper picks it up. "A Rubik's cube?"

I study it in her hand, the woman that is now holding a piece of me, the way I control my mind, an explanation of which exposes weakness. I could say what I say to everyone and I do just that. "It helps me focus," but unlike the rest of the world, she doesn't stop there.

"You're a savant," she says. "I read up on it. Most savants have time when the data in their heads takes over, when it overwhelms them and comes too fast. I even read about a man that has seizures when that happens."

She tried to pull back downstairs, to place a wall between us. I fight the urge to do the same now. I don't want to pull back with Harper and so I tell her what only Grayson and a few doctors know. "I collapsed in a swell of numbers when my mother died. My father paid for expensive doctors and one of them actually helped me, but when I got pulled up to law school three years early, and with Isaac, he was angry. He tried to trigger my episodes, as someone started calling them, but it's like the harder he tried, the stronger I got and the more desperate he became."

"And when you could have ruined him, you didn't," she says, repeating what I'd told her earlier.

"That's right. And joining the SEALs was good for me. They helped me hone my skills and turn them into assets, not detriments."

Her cellphone buzzes with a message on my side of the bed and she climbs over the top of me and ends up straddling my lap. "I need my phone. You were in the way."

I lean against the headboard, easing her body to mine. "Do you see me complaining?"

Her hand goes to my face, returning to our conversation. "Do you tell people you're a savant?"

"No. Never."

"Does it bother you that I know?"

"No, it doesn't. I don't announce what I am, but I own it."

"When was the last time you had an episode?"

I cover her hand with mine, tension sliding down my spine. "Why, Harper?"

"You don't have to tell me. Sorry." She tries to get off of me and I hold onto her.

"Why, Harper?" I ask again, intent on getting an answer from her.

"I just—if something happened, if you had one, if being here triggers one, I want to know how to help. I want to know what to do and what not to do."

I'm aware on every level that this is information she could use to hurt me. But I can't seem to home in on that part of the equation. No one has ever asked me what to do or not do besides my mother. "This," I say, dragging her mouth a breath from mine. "Kiss me, and kiss me with all you are."

She presses her lips to mine and her cellphone starts to ring this time. She groans and settles her forehead to mine, her hand on my jaw. "Twenty dollars of your billion says that will be my mother."

I'm struck by her ability to talk about my money and have it not feel like a play for my money. That's the thing about having money, I've learned. It comes with agendas, other people's agendas.

"Talk to her," I say, stroking her hair. "I'll be here when you're done."

"Let me just make sure it's her." She leans to the nightstand and grabs her phone and almost falls. She yelps and I catch her, helping her settle back on top of me. "Yep," she says. "It's her. I think I need that wine we didn't finish to survive her tonight."

I roll her to her back. "I'll get it." I kiss her and stand up, walking toward the door as her phone stops ringing without her answering it.

I turn to find her staring at me. "Sorry."

"Don't apologize. Talk to your mom."

"Not just about the interruption again. About how she acted earlier, Eric. You're being really great about her and she doesn't deserve it."

"You already said all this."

"I know. I just needed to say it again."

I soften with her concern, and I wonder how anyone that thinks about everyone else the way she does, me especially, has made it this long in this family. "Talk to your mom," I order playfully and head down the stairs.

Once I'm at the bottom of the stairs, I punch in a text to Adam, who I've had in my phonebook since a job Walker did for Bennett Enterprises a few months back: *How do we look out there?*

Like we're both in Denver instead of New York City, he replies. In other words, he's a smart ass and everything is clear. I walk into the living room, snag our wine glasses and the bottle and head back upstairs, ready to dig into the data Blake sent me before grabbing a few hours of sleep.

I re-enter the bedroom to find Harper missing and the bathroom door shut. I walk to the bed, set down our glasses and fill them before I sit down myself to wait on her, keying my MacBook to life. It's just about ready for use when Harper's phone buzzes on the bed next to me. My gaze lifts instinctively and lands on a flashing text message from Gigi that says: *Do not tell him.*

CHAPTER THIRTY-SIX

Eric

I'm standing at the bathroom door, my arm resting on the jamb when Harper opens it. She jolts. "Eric."

"Start talking, Harper. No more fucking lies."

"You read my text messages," she says, and it's not a question. She knows I did, but I go ahead and drive that point all the fucking way home.

"Damn straight I did," I say. "You left your phone on the bed to flash right at me."

"If I wasn't going to tell you, do you think I'd leave my phone on the bed?" she challenges and yanks her phone from my hand and starts reading. "*He has to know everything. You wanted him here. I'm telling him.*" She looks at me. "Does that sound like I had something to keep from you?"

"Looks to me like you ran to the bathroom to pull yourself together."

"I had to pee, Eric. I'm human like that. Do you want to listen to me or are you just going to attack?"

"Talk."

"I sent Gigi the message and she freaked out. She thinks it's a wire transfer number that points to her. She said she had wires into her account that were large and random. Isaac said they were bonuses, but then he asked for the money back as loans. And for the record, she just told me this. I didn't have a secret to keep. I just found out." She tries to duck around me.

I catch both of her wrists and pull her to me. "Why the fuck are you telling Gigi anything?"

"I thought she might know what the sequence was. I thought she could help."

"Don't tell Gigi anything you don't talk to me about first. Do you understand?"

She sucks in a breath and nods. "Yes," she whispers. "I get it. You hate her. You have reason to hate her. I just—"

"Don't say another word. I don't want to hear anything but your promise that it won't happen again because I want to trust you, Harper, but I can't if you're with her."

"I'm not. I'm not with her. You know that. We've talked about this."

"And yet you were texting with her about the note."

"I was trying to help. I thought—I thought she could help."

I stare down at her, searching her eyes for the truth that is hers, but all I find is the one that's mine. I release her and leave her there, exiting the bedroom to the hallway and my hands come down on the railing, the past playing in my mind. Gigi. That fucking bitch Gigi. I squeeze my eyes shut with a flashback, me at sixteen, my mother barely forty and sick, but all she thought of was me. I'd gotten a ride home from a buddy. I'm back there now and I never go there:

Kevin pulls his Jeep into the drive, in front of our trailer that seems more broken down these days since my mother got sick. "Who's the old lady with your mom?" Kevin asks of the woman standing with my mom on the wooden porch a neighbor built us a few years back.

The answer to that question punches me in the chest and I stare, squeezing the stress ball in my hand that the special teacher I'm seeing swears will calm my mind. "No idea," I say, squeezing harder now, fighting the assault of numbers threatening my mind, "but the church has been coming around a lot lately."

"They helping you guys?"

I shrug and crush the ball, holding onto it. "I guess. See you tomorrow." I open the door and get out, slamming the door behind me, and worried my mother needs my support, I head up the stairs.

A wrinkled woman with orange-ish hair is standing in profile to me, facing my mother, and God, my mother looks so thin. She hugs herself and speaks to the woman. "You need to leave."

"Mom?" I say, uncertain about this reaction. My mother is a kind person. She doesn't speak to people like that.

The old lady turns her attention to me. "Is this the little bastard you want to call a Kingston?" She looks me up and down before eyeing my mother. "He's no Kingston. He will never be a Kingston. Stay away, you little con artist." She charges down the steps, passing me, and when my eyes meet my mother's, I see the pain slicing through her stare.

I rotate and charge after the old lady. "My mom is no con artist. She's dying, you bitch! You're horrible. Who are you?"

"No one you will ever know. No one to you ever. Remember that in case she doesn't. You are nothing. You will never be anything to me or us." She climbs in the car and I rotate again and run toward my mother who is now inside the trailer.

I enter to find her waiting for me, her arms folded in front of her chest again. "We need to talk," she says.

I shut the door. "Who was that woman?"

"I have lied to you your entire life."

I clutch the ball in my hand. "What?"

"Your father wasn't a Navy SEAL. He didn't die serving his country. That was your uncle, my youngest brother."

"I don't understand."

She grabs another stress ball from the bar behind her and walks to me, pressing it into my free hand. "I had an affair. I slept with a married man, but I swear I didn't know he was married until I was pregnant. He called me a slut and liar and—" She sobs and covers her face with her hands.

I know on some level I should comfort her, but I can't do it. Numbers begin to stream and speak to me, they speak in ways I can't explain, in ways I can't calm. They tell me what to ask, what to think. "Who was that woman?"

"Your grandmother. You're a Kingston, son, and before I die, you will be claimed. That will be my gift to you. A ticket out of this hellhole."

My temples start to throb and data punches at my mind like fists on a bag. I start to lose reality and I can't hold onto the balls anymore. I try. I try to squeeze them, but they tumble to the ground. I can't think. I can't see beyond what the numbers want to say to me. I sink to my knees and in the depths of thousands of numbers, I see only one thing. That old lady with the red hair's disdainful look as she'd looked at my mother and called her a con artist right before she turned her attention to me, "The little bastard?"

I blink back to the present, my knuckles white where I hold the banister. I'm not a little bastard now. I'm a big fucking bastard that could hurt that woman. Harper slides under my arms in front of me, her hand settling on my chest, heat radiating from her palm and down my arms. "I'm sorry," she says. "She just—"

"Choose now. Her or me."

"You," she says immediately. "There's no question there. *You, Eric.* If you would have given me the chance, I would have shown you that a long time ago."

"You were always one of them."

Pain darts through her eyes. "I was never one of them, but clearly I'm a fool. You'll never believe that." She tries to duck under my arms again and my leg captures hers, blocking her way.

"Actions speak louder than words."

"Exactly," she says. "I made a mistake tonight. I know that, but you give me no room to be human. I'm perfect or I'm a Kingston. I can't do this. I can't feel what I feel for you and have you destroy me the way you want to destroy them." She tries to move away again but I don't even think about letting her free.

"Let me go," she demands, her voice trembling. "Let me go and maybe this time I'll have the reality check to finally let you go."

"What do you feel, Harper?"

"Anger."

I cup her face and cage her against the railing, my legs shackling hers. "You said you can't feel what you feel if I'm going to destroy you. What do you feel?"

"Too damn much for a man who doesn't even know his own hatred. For a man who wants to destroy everyone attached to this family, and that means me."

"If anyone can destroy anyone, it's you. You could, if I gave you the opportunity, if I trusted you enough, you could destroy me like no one else ever dreamt of destroying me."

"*If* you trust me? Because you don't?"

"Why should I give you that power? Why, Harper?"

"Because," she whispers, her voice a rasp of emotion, "if you don't, then it's too much. *My* too much is just that—too much and I can't do this."

Her words radiate through me and shift something inside me. I need this woman and damn it, I know she could destroy me, but the bottom line is I don't fucking care. "And if too much isn't enough?" I demand, twining her hair around my hand.

"Stop pushing me away."

"Does this feel like I'm pushing you away?" I cover her mouth with mine, and I don't just kiss her. I demand more, because I finally understand the way Grayson craves his woman, the way he will do anything for her, risk anything for her. There is no such thing as too much with this woman; even if she does destroy me in the end.

CHAPTER THIRTY-SEVEN

Harper

With the banister at my back and Eric in front of me, kissing me, his hands all over my body, it's like something has snapped between us. It's a matter of seconds, it seems, before my pants are off and his are open, a condom in his hand. It's the condom that gets to me again, driving home how much I need to talk to him about certain things I haven't yet, but now doesn't feel like the time. Now *really* isn't the time because he's already kissing me again, lifting my knee to his hip and pressing inside me.

Another few seconds and he's lifting me instead of my leg, cupping my backside. My legs wrap around his hips, and he's holding my weight, thrusting into me even as he kisses me. His tongue thrusting deep like his cock, and this is no gentle encounter between us. It's wild, fast and hard and we're both shuddering to release far too quickly, and yet it's somehow perfect. I come back to reality with my face in his neck and he's carrying me to the bathroom. He sits me on the sink and presses his hands on the counter on either side of me, anger burning in his eyes that sex clearly did nothing to tame. In fact, if anything, the opposite. He's angrier now, like he's pissed that he wanted and needed to fuck me. "Eric—"

"Me or Gigi," he says roughly, his face all hard lines and shadows.

"You. *You*, Eric. You can read the messages. All of them."

"I will. Don't tell her anything without talking to me first."

"I won't."

He pulls out of me and tosses the condom in a trashcan, scrubbing his jaw before he looks at me. "You do know she could be setting you up, right?"

"I know what she's capable of," I say. "I was going to tell you what she said." I hop off the counter. "I want you to read the messages." I start walking and he shackles my wrist and pulls me back to him.

"I need to be able to trust you, Harper. There is no in between for us."

"You can. I swear to you, Eric, on my father's life, on all that I am, that you can trust me. I'm sorry. You went downstairs and she texted me to see if we had any news and I just—I asked her about the number."

"How long have you known about the wire transfers?"

"Just read the messages, Eric. I want to get you my phone."

He reaches into his pocket and produces my phone. "I have it, remember?"

"Right. Good. Read the messages. Read any of my messages."

His stares at me, ignoring the messages, searching my face, and I don't look away. I want him to see the truth in my eyes. "I will not ever go to Gigi or anyone without talking to you first. I know what she did to you and your mom. I should have thought—"

"Yes. You should have." He releases me and walks into the bedroom. I grab my pink silk robe from behind the door and quickly slip it on, entering the bedroom as he sits on one of the chairs and starts reading through my messages.

I cross to sit in the chair angled his direction, right across from him. He finishes the thread with Gigi and then hands me my phone and reaches for his. He punches in an auto-dial and then it starts ringing on speakerphone. "Blake," he says when a man answers. "Meet Harper."

"How the fuck are you, Harper?"

I laugh. "Well you made me laugh, but otherwise"—my eyes meet Eric's—"I'm not very fucking good, actually."

"Talk to me," he says. "I'm everyone's therapist. Well, my wife's at least, or maybe she's mine."

Eric leans toward me, his elbows on his knees. "Gigi freaked out when Harper told her about the message we got tonight. She thought it was a wire transfer number. Seems she's been getting some large wires and then pulling the cash for Isaac."

"Indeed she has," he says. "I sent you proof of those transactions. As for her pulling the cash and giving it to Isaac, I reserve judgment on that idea. If I can't prove it, I don't believe it."

"Agreed," Eric says. "What do you know about the wires she's been getting?"

"The identifier as you called it, is not a bank transaction, a foreign exchange number, or anything that pulls up electronically with any ease at all. I'll dig into personal emails and documents over the next few days. I'll let you know what I find."

Eric eyes me. "Questions for Blake?"

"A very broad one. Do you have any idea what's going on?"

"A cover-up for sure," he says. "My concern is that it could be a set-up with Eric as the target."

"I'm not setting him up. Eric, I'm not setting you up. I'm not part of this."

"We'll talk later, Blake," Eric says, disconnecting the line. "I know you're not setting me up, but *they* may be setting me up through you and I can't allow that to touch Grayson Bennett. He's been too damn good to me."

Panic rushes over me and I pop to my feet. Eric is there with me, his hands settling on my arms. "I'm not going to let them hurt me or you. I'm here. I have a world of resources, which means you have a world of resources."

"There's something weird about Isaac having me take over this union negotiation."

"Meaning what?"

"Involving me came out of nowhere. It's not what I do and it could have been to keep me busy, but it feels like more. My instinct, the first thing that came to my mind, was that he was setting me up in some way."

"Never disregard your instincts," he says. "And I'd already planned on going to the union meeting with you."

"Maybe that's the idea. Connect you and me to something unsavory. Don't go with me."

"I'm going with you, Harper. End of subject."

"Eric—"

He drags me closer and kisses me. "It'll be fine."

"We don't even know what's going on. We don't know where the bullets are coming from. Blake's assumption feels right. This is a set-up. I brought you into a set-up. You have to leave."

"I'll leave if you'll come with me."

"You know I can't do that."

"Then I'm staying."

"I'm a bad person. I need to tell you that I'm a bad person."

His eyes narrow, and I feel the slight stiffening in his body next to mine. "What does that mean, Harper?"

"The honorable thing to do right now is to make you leave."

His expression softens. "You can't make me leave."

I wish that was true, I think. I wish so much that I didn't have a secret that would make him hate me. I tell myself to tell him now, but it's embarrassing and I'm ashamed that I didn't handle a piece of my life, of *his* life, in a better way. He'll leave when he finds out. He'll go home and that means he'll be out of this. He'll be protected and I care about this man. I need to suck it up and take the hate. I need to force him to leave. I need to just tell him. I need to do it now.

But then he strokes my hair in that way he does that is both tender and sensual, and it undoes me. "We're in this together, Harper," he says with that warm, gravelly tone of his that is sex and sin and friendship all in one. "Which is why," he adds, "we're going to get comfortable, drink wine, and dig through the data Blake gave us. Together. We're going to do this together. Say it."

"Together," I repeat, and I like this word for us. I like it so much that I'm selfish. I can't tell him right this minute. I'll tell him tomorrow. I'll tell him everything in the morning.

CHAPTER THIRTY-EIGHT

Eric

With the word "together" between us, I reach up and untie the sash of Harper's pink silk robe and then turn her to face the door, dragging it down her shoulders, letting the silk pool at our feet. "Let's get comfortable and get to work," I say, my lips by her ear, my fingers catching on her shirt, and pulling it over her head.

"And that requires I be naked?" she asks.

I remove my shirt and slip it over her head, the material falling past her knees as I turn her to face me and she slips her arms into the sleeves. "My way of reminding you that we're together as we dig into the investigation. Together, Harper."

"Together doesn't mean jumping to conclusions like you did over Gigi without talking to me first."

"I'll concede that to be true," I say. "And I'm *sorry*."

She blanches. "You're sorry?"

"Yes," I say. "I'm sorry, and in case you didn't know, savants are good at apologizing, in my case, if it mathematically makes sense."

It's a joke, but she doesn't laugh.

"You're not going to say anything more about the Gigi incident?"

"I believe you had good intentions," I say, and I do. "I believe you'll talk to me next time first."

"I will. I promise."

"Then let's put it behind us. That's mathematically logical as well."

She smiles. "I like this mathematically logical stuff you do."

"Good, because it's who I am, sweetheart." I glance at my black and silver TAG Heuer watch, one of the first expensive things I bought myself, and then back to her. "It's ten. I want to analyze the data Blake sent me and have you show me the data you collected before we catch a few hours of sleep."

"Of course," she says. "I have a paper file I put together. I was paranoid about the electronic data getting wiped out or it being discovered by the wrong people." She moves to the side of the bed where she's taken up residence for the night, and I claim my spot as she pulls a folder from her briefcase.

"This is what I've pulled together, but honestly, I'm not sure it helps much. It tells us there's funny stuff going on but we know that already and it's nothing." Her cellphone rings again and she glances at the caller ID. "My mother," she confirms. "I'm taking it on speaker. My reminder to you that I'm with you." She doesn't give me time to approve or object. She answers the line.

"Hi, mom."

"He's still there with you, isn't he?"

"Yes," Harper confirms, glancing at me as she adds, "He is. We're together. We're seeing each other."

"He's your stepbrother. That's embarrassing."

Harper reacts about the same way I did to Isaac issuing that same jab. Irritation flits across her face and she snaps back. "We're adults that never even lived together and I can't even believe you went there. You're married to a man who out ages you by a huge number. I know how sensitive you are to that, but when it's me you're going to attack?"

"Your father—"

"Okay, mom. This is more of the same conversation we had when you were here tonight. He's not my father, and frankly, I'm tired of you dishonoring my real father, the man that was supposed to be your soul mate, by calling Jeff my father. I'm not going to say more. Right now, you're not in a state of mind to listen."

She's silent for several beats. "There are things about Eric you don't know. I need you to hear those things before you continue down this destructive path."

"I'm going to let Eric tell me about Eric. Just like I want him to let me be the one to tell him about me."

"When your fath— Jeff, gets here tomorrow, you're going to have to talk to him about Eric."

"Jeff needs to talk to Eric," Harper says, "*his son*, which is what I will tell him."

His son.

Fuck, I hate the way that reference cuts. I didn't think it could cut anymore, but it does.

Harper's mother is silent for several beats. "I beg of you, daughter, please don't do this."

"I'm protecting you," Harper says. "One day you'll thank me." Her mother sobs and hangs up.

Harper sets the phone on the bed. "I'm all for digging into the data." She grabs my cube. "I can never work these things. Can you?"

I take it from her, use a few rotations of my hand and solve the puzzle before setting it down. "Talk to me."

She turns her stare on me and for several beats she just searches my face, just looks at me. "What if I don't know her anymore, Eric? What if she's one of them now? What if she knows what's going on and has willingly stayed involved?"

I lean forward and stroke a strand of hair from her eyes. "Then you save her anyway. She's your mother."

"That's not what you said when I told you I had to save her."

"I changed my mind."

"Why?" she asks, covering my hand with hers.

"Because, sweetheart, I wanted to save my mother from this family and I couldn't." It's a confession I've made to no one, ever. "Just like your mother, she didn't want to be saved."

"Your mother was trying to save you, not herself. That's different. She did what she did out of love for you. Mine. Mine doesn't seem to care about me at all."

"Or she's desperate to protect you," I suggest. "She wants you to back off before someone hurts you. Give her the benefit of the doubt."

"Thank you, Eric. I know that you're seeing her in a different light to help me. It really matters."

"Yeah, well, sweetheart, I wouldn't have gotten so damn pissed at you over Gigi if you didn't matter to me. Trust is everything to me."

She sucks in a breath and glances away before looking at me. "Because this family hurt you so badly."

"They cut me, but I don't bleed easily, not anymore." Her phone buzzes with a text and she glances down at it and then shows it to me. It's from Gigi and it reads: *Answer me, Harper. Do not tell Eric.*

I study it a few beats and look at Harper. "I'm not objective about Gigi. I hate her and I don't hate easily. Tell her okay, you won't tell me. Give her space to feel safe and we'll sit back and see what she does next." I wait for Harper to reject this directive, but she doesn't.

She types a message and shows it to me. It reads almost identical to what I suggested she say, but she hasn't pressed send yet. "Good?" she asks.

"Good," I approve.

She hits send and sets her phone aside. "I don't have the capacity to wade through information with the same results you can, but let me help. What can I do?"

"Show me your file and explain what concerns you."

From there, we dig in, and after reviewing her data with me, she starts reading through the files Blake sent me. In the midst of it all, I tease another investor on the NFL deal, refuse calls from Julius, the asshole trying to set-up the deal, and ensure Grayson knows what card I'm playing. It's one in the morning when Harper is snuggled next to me, sound asleep, and I move her MacBook to the nightstand. With her pressed to my side, I continue to work, and I decide that I could damn sure get used to this woman by my side, in a bed, any bed, with me.

I flip through her data again, my Rubik's cube in my hand, and I compare the data to the files that were deleted from Kingston's systems, homing in on Isaac's email when I set the cube down. He deleted every email to a man named Tim Carlson, who just so happens to be a high-ranking officer of the automobile union. And Harper is not only meeting with the union tomorrow, she feels like it's a set-up. I don't like how that looks, feels, or sounds, especially when Gigi, who I don't trust, befriended Harper and now she doesn't want me to know about cash deposits. But she wanted me here. She sent Harper to get me. Blake's right. Harper and I are being set-up.

CHAPTER THIRTY-NINE

Eric

I wake at sunrise with Harper pressed to my side, the heat of her body next to mine warming me in places I thought to be pure, unbreakable ice, but I was wrong. This woman chips away that ice, and while I didn't think I wanted it chipped away, now I want her warmth in all those cold places. She's changing me. She doesn't know it, but I do. With every moment that I'm with her, she seeps deeper inside me, and she was already there to begin with. She's been there for six illogical, but absolute, years. For a solid fifteen minutes, I lay there, just listening to her breathe, and when I finally force myself to get up to deal with a phone conference I've set up on the NFL deal, she sinks deeper into the covers, and to me, this represents trust. With all she has going on, with all the fears she's nursing, she feels safe with me here. And she is. No one is ever going to hurt her again.

I pull on my boots I took off hours ago, drag my jacket on without a shirt, stick the gun in the back of my jeans, and then head downstairs, exiting the house into a cold Denver morning to grab my garment bag from the trunk of my rental. I check in with Blake by text, despite talking to him a few hours ago, or rather texting with him. I re-enter the bedroom and Harper hasn't moved. I finishing showering and still, she hasn't moved. I shave and dress in a three-thousand-dollar suit, meant to represent Bennett Enterprises with the union today. I accessorize with the gun at the back of my pants, under my jacket. I make coffee and predict how Harper takes hers based on the supplies she has in the house and then head upstairs.

I set the cup on the nightstand and then settle my hand on Harper's arm. She blinks and brings me into focus. "Eric? God, is that really you?"

My lips curve at her sleepy, dreamy reaction. "Yes, sweetheart. It's really me. I brought you coffee."

She rockets to a sitting position. "Eric?"

I laugh. "Yes. It's still me."

"I was—I think I was—"

"Dreaming?"

"Yes. I was really asleep and I think and you were—It was just a dream."

Dreaming of me. Fuck. She's undoing me here. I should have come back for her. I never should have left her.

"Oh God," she says, grabbing my arm. "What time is it? I have that union meeting."

"It's only six-thirty." I offer her the coffee. "You have time."

"You really made me coffee?"

"I really made you coffee," I confirm as she accepts the cup and sips.

"And you made it how I like it. Was there some statistical reason you chose my perfect mixture?"

"I guessed based on how you stock your supplies."

"You did good," she approves, "and how very un-bastard-like of you." She eyes my suit. "You look really, really good in a suit. Actually, you look really, really good in a T-shirt. And apparently, I have no filter with you."

"No filter equals honesty. Keep it coming. And for the record, you look damn good in my shirt. You'd look better in my bed. I may have to go back to New York for a meeting on this NFL deal. Come with me."

She sets the coffee down. "I can't leave in the middle of this, but you, you need to leave before you get set-up in some way. I fell asleep thinking about that. You need to go."

"I'm not going anywhere without you. Come into my world, into my life, and be a part of it."

"Would that include you telling me what all your tattoos mean?"

"Yes, Harper. I'll tell you what my tattoos mean."

"That's tempting, really tempting and I wish I could, Eric, but I can't leave. You know I can't leave."

"You can," I say, and when she opens her mouth to object, I hold up a finger. "Hear me out, sweetheart."

She hesitates but nods before I continue, "We'll convince them that I gave you a reason to leave and backed you the hell out of this mess. In theory, they then let down their guards while the Walker team is hacking and watching."

"You really think that will work?"

"I know this family far better than I wish I did, Isaac especially. He is never smart about how he covers his tracks."

"He covered them well enough to keep us from uncovering them now."

"You've been in his face, you've been pushing him. Come to New York with me." My hand comes down on her leg. "Sleep in my bed with me. Live in my world with me. See what life outside the Kingston world is like. They've consumed you. And if you see it, if you love it, you'll sell it to your mom."

Her eyes soften. "I want to. God, I really want to."

"Then do it. Remove yourself from the target zone, too."

Worry pinches her brow. "Does that put my mother there instead?"

"We'll watch for trouble, but I don't see her as a target."

"How would that look? What would we do to set this up?"

"I'll go at them hard for a few days and you stay your course. Don't change how you've been acting at all. Don't say a word to Gigi about backing down. Then I'll pull back and tell my father that I'll bow out in exchange for your protection. I've walked away before. He'll believe me."

"You think it will work?"

"Yes, and I read my father well. I'll know when to play the cards if it's working."

She considers me several beats. "Me going to your home is our play?"

"Yes."

"Me in your bed?"

"The best fucking play ever," I assure her.

Her lips curve, her mood shifting to yes before she ever speaks it. "I have a condition," she says, her eyes lighting with mischief.

"What condition?"

"Every tattoo I lick, you explain."

I laugh and kiss her hand. "Condition accepted and feel free to start that process before we get to New York and my bed."

"A suggestion worthy of consideration."

I lean in and cup her head, dragging her lips to mine. "How about I lick *you* all over instead?"

"Can we take turns?"

I kiss her, and the throb of my cock is instant, while my conference call is imminent, and it's all I can do to leave her in her bed, all but naked in my shirt. But I do, and only because soon she'll be in my bed where she'll stay naked.

Harper

I have to tell him my secret before I can go to New York with him. I have to. I will. It's the right thing to do. It's the only thing to do. These are the thoughts in my head as I dress in a black dress and thigh-high tights with lace tops, my mind is racing the entire time I go through my morning routine. I am falling hard for this man. I have been from the day I met him and now, we're here, we're together, we're doing this, and the past hangs over our heads. The consequences of our first night together reach far beyond what Eric believes to be the reality.

I grab my purse and briefcase and head downstairs, following the echo of Eric's deep, sexy voice to the kitchen. I find him at the island, coffee cup in hand, his MacBook open on the counter, while the phone is at his ear. His tattoos peek from beneath his sleeve, a canvas of all the lives he's lived and I want to know them all. I want this secret not to destroy us, but not telling him isn't an option. We said no secrets and this one isn't one I could live with holding back.

I approach the island and he looks up, his eyes warming with the sight of me in that way every girl wants a man of her heart to look at her with. And he is the man of my heart. I am falling in love with him. I have always been standing on a ledge above a sea of wild blue love with this man, ready to jump. But I can't jump and have that water become ice.

"Let me call you back, Blake," Eric says, disconnecting and shutting his computer, his eyes doing a wicked glide up and down my body. "You look beautiful, Harper."

"Thank you," I say stopping at the island across from him and it's the wrong time. I know it's the wrong time, but when I look into his eyes, when the warmth of his stare radiates through me, I can barely contain this explosion inside me. "Eric, I need—"

Both of our cellphones ring at the same time. Eric winks and my moment of poorly timed confession is gone. We both reach for our phones. Mine turns out to be Jim Sims. "Jim," I greet. "We're still on for our meeting this morning, right? At the union office?"

"No meeting."

"Why?"

"Isaac and I talked last night. We agreed on terms."

"Just like that?"

"It's done. No meeting." He hangs up without another word.

I frown and slide my phone into my purse as Eric disconnects, arching a brow at me. "What just happened?"

"The union meeting is cancelled. They agreed to our terms. So actually, I'm turning your question on you. What just happened?"

"Isaac deleted the union messages when I walked in the door. Now the meeting between you and the union is cancelled. Kingston's obviously in bed with at least a portion of the union. My presence and history with the union has everyone spooked. Add to that the fact that my father just called and demanded to see me at the office right now and I'd say our plan is working. The one where we leave and you end up in my bed."

Unless I don't, I think. Unless he decides he doesn't want me there, because I can't go to New York City without telling him what I don't want to tell him. What I have to tell him.

CHAPTER FORTY

Harper

Eric pulls us into the Kingston parking lot in his Jaguar rental after we decided to ride to work together, which is the part I'm fine with. The choice of car is another story. "I can't believe we're in a Jaguar," I say. "I work for Kingston."

"You're making a statement," he says yet again, since we had this debate at my house. "The Kingstons don't own us. They don't own you. And that's an important message. It's the one that puts pressure on them. It's the one that makes them feel relief when I convince you to leave."

"Right," I say. "I know you're right." But the idea that his father will be here today, and get in my face, is not a good one. Isaac I can deal with. He's an ass that makes you hate him. Jeff is another story. My stepfather has a way of crawling under your skin and cutting from the inside.

Eric turns me to face him. "You've been their 'yes' girl for six years."

I scowl at him. "I'm the one who's been in their faces about the recalls and funny money. I'm the reason you're here."

"But for six years, you played a role in the company, you played the good little employee. And you did it so well that no one thought twice about using your trust fund."

"My mother allowed that," I say. "I still can't believe she allowed that to happen."

"Here's what you need to remember, sweetheart. Your father didn't believe she'd let it happen. He believed he took care of you. Your mother has changed, she's inside the Kingston web."

"Yes, but—"

"I know you want to save her, but you don't save someone by ignoring what you're saving them from. She's brainwashed and that means she will act to protect them and convince herself that's in your best interest even if it's not. She burned you. She will burn you again if you let her. Understand?"

I flash back to the night I found out she gave my stepfather my trust fund. We were at one of our mother-daughter Sunday brunches we do once a month, sipping coffee and eating waffles:

"I need to share something exciting," my mother says, setting her coffee aside.

I sip from my cup and do the same. "Exciting is good. I'm all ears."

"Jeff is going to invest your trust fund and he's assured me you'll get a twenty-percent return."

I blanch. "What? What does that mean?"

"He says that seven million dollars shouldn't just sit when it could be earning money for the company your father helped build and for you. I gave him the money a month ago, and he says it's already earning you ten percent more than the way it was banked."

"You did what?"

"This is great news, honey."

"How did you do this? That money is in my name."

"I'm the executor and—"

"I'll never see that money back again." I lean forward and all but growl. "What have you done? How could you do this to me?"

"Harper?"

I blinked back to the present and into Eric's blue eyes. "Where were you just now?"

"Remembering the day my mother told me she gave my trust fund to Jeff and how great it was going to be for me."

"What did you say?"

"I was angry. I knew I'd never see the money again. I started looking for a job then. I wanted out, but unlike her with me, I put her first. I stayed when the fatalities happened to protect her. But you're right. She's brainwashed. I think she really believes I don't appreciate what Jeff does for me."

"My father is a master manipulator and she wants to be manipulated by him."

I tilt my head to look at him. "I'm surprised you call him your father."

"My mother told me that I had to own what I wanted."

"And you wanted him to be your father?"

"I wanted what my mother wanted. For him to claim me as his son, but that was a long time ago and he told me to call him father. Of course, he was trying to push Isaac to step up. He was using me."

"And you still address him as father?"

"Every time I call him father, I remind him that my mother was never a person to be ignored." Shadows flit through his stare before he refocuses on me and his cellphone buzzes with a text. He snakes it from his pocket and reads the message before replying and updating me. "Blake hacked all the recording devices in the building but didn't install his own. He said after careful consideration and review of the camera placement with more detail, he has full access, which means whatever is said in this building he'll hear."

I know the answer already, but I just need to confirm. I need to hope. "My office was for sure recorded, right?"

"Yes," he says stroking my cheek. "I know you hate that they saw you change clothes."

"Yes, well, just another reason to kick your brother and father in the balls, even if it's a proverbial kick."

"That's my girl," he says, the endearment doing funny things to my belly. "Lead the conversations you have where you want them to go. Everything you get the family to say while we have access to the recordings could be useful if we need to protect your interests."

"And innocence?"

"They won't frame you or me for their crimes. That's not going to happen. Let them move things around while we watch. Then when we leave, they'll make bigger moves."

"We hope."

"We expect," he says. "My father flew back because I'm here. They feel the pressure. I'm going to ensure they feel it ten times over. And when he comes at you, you do the same. That's our plan. Stick with it."

"I know. I will."

He kisses me. "I'll come around and get you." He opens his door and exits. I gather my briefcase and by the time I have my purse stuffed inside it, Eric is opening my door and offering me his hand.

I slide my palm to his, and I swear every time this man touches me, I light up. I'm alive in ways I didn't realize I could be alive, in ways I want to be for the rest of my life, and that's a scary thought. This man could hurt me, and that has nothing to do with the company or the family. It's all about us and what I feel for him that I'm afraid to name. I need to just enjoy him, and love the time with him. I need to live in the now.

"Whatever you're feeling," he says softly, walking me to him, "I am, too."

My gaze rockets to his and he brushes his knuckles over my cheek. "I'd tell you what I feel if we weren't here in this Godforsaken place." He settles my hand on his elbow, and unlike me, he's not wearing a coat. "There's much to talk about, Harper. Alone. In New York City. Away from this place. Today helps us get there. Let's go do this."

"Yes. Let's go do this."

He turns us toward the building, and arm in arm we walk to the main entrance, our relationship on full display. Eric opens the door for me and nerves assail me. His father is here. He's going to confront me. My mother is going to confront me. Isaac and Gigi, too. But they'll go at Eric as well, and that's what we want.

I enter the lobby first but Eric is immediately back by my side. The receptionist stares at us a minute before she says, "Gigi wants to see you."

I'd expected as much, but it's then that I realize Eric and I haven't talked about what I'm going to say to Gigi. "Tell her I'll find her when I get settled."

The receptionist clears her throat. "Sorry. I meant Eric. She wants to see you, Eric."

"I'm sure she does," he says, glancing first at a text message, and then at me, before motioning for me to step back outside.

I nod and follow him to the right and down the stairs. As soon as we're behind closed doors, he turns and faces me, drags me to him and whispers in my ear. "Treat Gigi likes she's setting you up. Get her to talk."

"Yes. Yes, okay."

The doors behind us open and Eric rotates us to face the door, where his father has just entered the room, no doubt having witnessed our embrace.

CHAPTER FORTY-ONE

Eric

I stand toe to toe with my father, a man who we all know looks more like me than Isaac, and that hasn't changed. He's tall, athletic, his eyes the same blue as mine, his hair now streaked with gray, but still the same wavy brown. All details that feed Isaac's insecurity and bitterness. As for my genius, per Gigi, that's her doing, a detail I just don't care enough about to research.

"Father," I say, tightly.

"Leave us, Harper," he orders without looking at her.

I grab her and meet her stare. "I'm here if you need me."

"I'm here if you need me," she replies.

Holy hell, this woman charms the fuck out of me. I barely contain a smile at her reply, but I manage to give her a nod and release her. She walks around my father and exits the conference room. "Are you going to tell me what you're doing to get people killed while they're driving your cars, or give me a few more days that might only take hours to figure it out myself?"

"You don't belong here."

"I'm family, blood, *your son*. If any of that mattered to me, I'd be offended. What matters is money. Gigi paid me to find out what you won't tell her."

"Gigi is old and senile and we both know you have more money than God. You don't need her pathetic money."

"Any man that makes money and keeps that money values it. She's concerned enough to make it worth my while, but let's get real here. Harper is why I'm here. You hurt her, I hurt you. That's the bottom line."

"Your stepsister."

"Who I'm fucking, yes. Now that we're past the taboo part of that equation, you're in trouble. We both know you're in trouble. Trust your son to help."

"We aren't in trouble, *son*. Harper's pissed off about us using her trust fund and you're letting her grab your balls and pull you around."

"Harper doesn't need that trust fund. She has me and you of all people know that I know how to turn money into more money."

"We'll pay you off," he says. "Go back to New York City."

"I'm a stockholder now. I'm not going anywhere, and with Gigi's stock offered up for my purchase, if you push me too hard, I'll take the majority, and you might be the one who's gone."

His lips quirk. "You had your chance. You walked away."

"As if you ever wanted me to run this place."

"I wanted the best man to win and the one that ran away wasn't the best man."

"I didn't run," I say. "I stepped outside your limitations. Now you're confined to your mistakes and we both know you've made them. Suck up the pride and let me help while it's still possible to save this place."

"Just like your mother. You think you can arm yourself with some small weapon and control me. I don't do anything I don't want to do, including claiming you as my son."

"You claimed me to fuck with Isaac. I wonder now if it's him that got you in trouble or vice versa. Did your crown prince endanger your empire? Or maybe you two dared down this path on your own."

"You're playing with matches, Eric. Don't light the match because you'll be the one who burns. I brought you into this world, I quite literally can take you out."

"Who will end who?" I say. "Is that the new game you're playing and are you really sure it's one you want to play with me?"

"I might not be able to beat you, son, but I don't have to beat you. There are others that will do it for me."

He turns and leaves. I stare at the door as it closes. I stare after the man who's supposed to be my only living parent, yet he just threatened to end me. And unlike my pussy brother, I believe he'd act on that threat, but there's a theme here between the two of them. Someone else is involved. Someone who will kill me. Someone who thinks they have the skills to do it despite my skills. They don't, but I want Harper the fuck out of here and then I need to end this family before they have the chance to come after her.

My cellphone buzzes with a text and Blake taps me into Harper's office and I know why. Gigi enters her office.

Harper

I've barely sat down at my desk when Gigi walks into my office and shuts the door, her red hair a mess she never allows it to be. "You told him?" she demands. "Did you tell him?"

I stand up and lean on my desk. "Why didn't you tell me? Wires into your account that you pulled out and gave Isaac. It looks like you're helping them and setting him up. You made it look like I was setting him up."

"I did what I had to do!" she shouts, shocking me with her outburst. "He wouldn't have come here to help if I told you because you wouldn't have helped me and gone to him."

"Why would you pull cash and give Isaac that money? What is really going on here?"

She charges toward my desk but I don't miss how unsteady she is as she does. She presses her hands on the opposite side of the desk. "I thought I was helping my grandson."

"Like you tried to get rid of your other grandson? You hurt Eric. Now you want him to help you without knowing the facts?"

"I can't undo the past. I can't. I told you. I regret what a bitch I was to him and his mother. I have nightmares about her suicide. I know what I did to her." She starts crying, deep sobs. "I don't know how to fix any of this."

"Start by walking up to him and telling him you're sorry."

"That won't matter to him."

"That doesn't mean he doesn't deserve it. He deserves it."

"And when looking at me disgusts him so much he leaves?" she demands. "Then what? He's going to take me down with them, isn't he?"

I could tell her no, I could tell her how honorable he is, and how much his mother inspired his actions. How much the Bennett family grounds him, but I don't. She doesn't deserve that security and I don't trust her not to repeat it anyway. "Holding back information from him certainly isn't the way to inspire his kindness."

"You're the only one who can inspire his kindness. I know you're seeing him. I know you were with him years ago at the party. I saw you go to his cottage. Protect me. Please."

I feel manipulated. I feel used. "Tell him everything. That's how you protect yourself. I can't. I won't. He deserves more than me using our relationship as a tool or a weapon."

She stares at me for several long beats and then walks toward the door. She pauses there and then exits without another word. The door shuts and I pray I've done my job right. My cellphone buzzes with a message from Eric: *I was watching and A) you scared her. That's good. What she does next could tell a story, but most importantly B) I really want to come in there and fuck you right there on your desk but there would be too many perverts watching. That doesn't work for me. I don't share. Not you. Ever.*

I smile and reply with: *Then I guess we'll have to use your desk in New York City when I go there with you.*

His reply is instant: *Yes, fucking yes, and if you keep talking like that I'll fire up a private jet and take you there now, tonight.*

Warmth fills me and for the first time, I really let myself believe that maybe, just maybe, we have a future and I'm willing to walk away from my past to make it happen. I'm willing to walk away for him. I want to walk away before this family does something to ruin us.

CHAPTER FORTY-TWO

Harper

It's nearly lunchtime and I've avoided any more encounters with the Kingston family. I spend the quiet time digging through every record I can find that might hold that fourteen-digit identifier we were given last night. It's noon when Eric appears in my doorway. "Want to grab lunch?"

"Yes, please. I'm suffocating in this place." I grab my purse and cross the office to greet him. He grabs my coat from the coat rack right inside my doorway, helps me into it, and then uses the lapels to pull me to him, kissing me soundly on the lips.

"How the hell does it feel like a year since I did that?" he murmurs against my mouth, his hand a warm branding on my lower back under my coat.

"Because it has been, right?" I ask sounding and feeling breathless. I live breathlessly with this man.

He laughs a low, sexy laugh that I feel from head to toe before he takes my hand and leads me toward the front desk. We enter the lobby at the same moment that Isaac walks in the front door. "Aren't they cute," he says dryly. "Fuck break or lunch break?" he asks in front of the receptionist.

Eric looks at me and arches a brow. "Lunch, right?"

His nonchalant, unruffled reply guides my equally unruffled reply. "Can we decide in the car?"

"Whatever you want, sweetheart," he says, leaning in to kiss me before he lifts a chin at Isaac. "Later, brother," he says, and we step outside into a gust of wind.

Eric pulls me under his arm. "Sorry about that in there," he says, glancing down at me. "He was looking for a reaction I didn't want to give."

"Me either," I say. "I'm glad you handled it like you did."

His eyes meet mine, and there is this swell of intimacy between us. There is no divide between us anymore. There is just us against them. The past is history. The future before us.

A few minutes later, we sit inside an Italian restaurant that specializes in pizzas, and once we place our orders, Eric updates me on the recent developments. "Gigi left the office with my father right after he and Isaac had this exchange." He offers me his phone and headset and I watch a short video that shows his father storming into Isaac's office, slamming the door shut and then going off on Isaac.

"*Clean up your mess and do it now,*" he bites out. "*Your brother is not an idiot, nor is he without resources.*"

"*Our mess,*" Isaac snaps. "*You sent me down this path.*"

"*I sent you down a dirt road. You turned it into a fucking highway.*"

"*Eric owns stock now. Gigi—*"

"*I'll deal with my mother. You clean it all up. Now.*"

The video ends and I slide the phone back to Eric. "I was right. It's something illegal."

"Yes," Eric confirms. "You were right."

"Any luck finding any clues to what this is all about?" I ask.

"Not yet, but I have a contact at the union in New York City. He owes me in a big way and he wanted inside the NFL deal. I called him. I told him he might have an in. We're meeting Monday."

"It's Wednesday," I remind him. "That's a long way off."

"I have to clear a path to get him into the NFL deal and that gives us more time to find out what the hell that message was about last night."

"I tried all morning with no luck. I think I need to go see my mother. I can search the house."

"Don't do that," he says. "Not while my father's in town. It's too dangerous." He leans in and cups my face. "Promise me."

I cover his hand on my face. "I promise."

"Let's go to New York tomorrow."

"So soon?"

"I need you out of here." His eyes meet mine, a storm of emotions in their depths, his voice low, gravelly, affected. "I cannot want you this damn badly, Harper, and have something happen to you."

Want me this damn badly.

Those words expand between us, wrap us in a warm awareness that says want is so much more than its obvious meaning. He's afraid of wanting me and losing me like he did his mother, like he did this family when they were his future. I understand him and in this moment, I feel him in every part of me. Something is happening between me and this man. He needs me and I need him and I don't know if that's forever but it's good, it's really good and right.

"I'm not going anywhere but with you to New York."

He kisses me, and it's a long, seductive kiss that ends when our pizza arrives, and we leave the Kingstons out of the rest of lunch. We talk about New York City and all the places he wants me to see and experience with him. It's perfect. It's just me and him, and it feels like coming home in a way I have never been home before.

Eric

I spend the afternoon in the conference room with the taste of Harper on my lips, the smell of her perfume on my clothes, and a mission on my mind: Get her the fuck out of here. I spend the bulk of the time that consumes our hours apart with the Rubik's cube in my hand, and the bank accounts for the company on my computer. Patterns emerge that I track back two years, movement of money that exposes wires to a bank account that I don't have a name to identify, but right now I focus on the numbers, just the numbers. Once I come out of my zone, I have a list of ten wires that I suspect were sent to Gigi, as the wires match those to the account I know to be hers. It's nearly six when I text Blake the number and ask for the owner of the account. His reply is instant: *Give me five minutes.*

I start reviewing more data and five minutes later exactly, Blake sends me a message: *Go outside and call me.*

I don't like the way that sounds and unease rolls through me, the idea that this could be related to Harper grinding a hole in my heart. This isn't about Harper. I need to fucking know what the hell is going on and I'm up the stairs in about thirty seconds, exiting the lobby in another thirty to step outside into what is becoming a bitter cold.

I dial Blake. He answers on the first ring. "The account is closed."

"Who owned it and please don't say Harper."

"The account had Harper and her mother on it."

Those words punch me in the fucking chest. "Who closed the account?"

"Harper."

"She knew about the wires then?"

"I don't know the answer to that question, but yes, I would assume she did."

My jaw tics. "I'll call you back."

I disconnect the line, walk back inside and head to the conference room where I pick up my Rubik's cube and I try like hell to calm my mind. I start turning it and turning it, casing every moment with Harper in numbers, in a way no one but me would understand. The numbers just keep fucking coming. Exactly an hour and thirty seconds have passed when I come back to reality and to three text messages from Harper that I don't answer. I need out of this office. I grab my things and head upstairs where the offices are closed up.

I exit to the parking lot into the darkness when it hits me that I rode with Harper. I'm about to turn back to the building and do what I should have already done; talk to her. I need to talk to her. Why the hell am I leaving? I'm two steps from the front door of the offices when Isaac joins me outside. "There he is, my brother." Isaac greets with a sneer that tells me he's up for games and nastiness and I'm not in the mood. "Coming back to get your woman?"

I ignore him and reach for the door when he says, "She needs you until she doesn't. She helps you until it doesn't work for her anymore. That's how she works."

The way he says that, like he knows her intimately, claws at me, and I take the bait I would never take if it wasn't Harper. I stop and turn around, numbers exploding in my mind in random bursts. "She won't help you now," I say. "No one will."

"She needed me once. Gigi told me you fucked her not long before that. She saw her go to your cottage. Then she came to me. Harper had a miscarriage, and fuck, it was a disaster. She is a disaster that started rumors. She bled out right here in the office. I took care of her the way you want to take care of her now. I wonder if the brothers thing gets her off." He smirks. "But I'm sure you don't care. You're just fucking her to fuck me, right?" He turns and starts walking toward his car.

Numbers pound at my mind again. I want them to replace the emotions that want to consume me. I try to open the lobby door, but I don't have an after-hours card. I dial Harper. "Come outside," I order when she answers. I disconnect before she can reply.

I lean on the wall, watching as Isaac drives away in his two-hundred-thousand-dollar special edition Kingston convertible. Harper exits, pulling her coat on as she does. "What's wrong?"

I grab her and pull her in front of me. "Did you fuck Isaac?"

"God no. No. No. We had this conversation. Where is this even coming from?"

"Did you have a miscarriage?"

She pales, her hand settling on her belly and I know even before she whispers. "I was going to tell you. I was—"

"What happened to no, you didn't fuck Isaac?" I challenge, those fucking numbers beating at my mind.

"It wasn't Isaac's. It was—I was going to call you but I—"

"Call me? We didn't even finish fucking, sweetheart. Why would you call me?" I don't give her time to reply. "Don't answer. I don't care. I'm gone. I'm done. Save yourself." I start walking and she screams after me. "Eric! Eric, wait."

I don't wait. I climb into my car, and she pounds on the window but I don't care. I meant what I said. I'm gone. I dial the airport, book a private jet, and head that direction. I can't get out of this city fast enough. I can't get away from *Harper* fast enough.

CHAPTER FORTY-THREE

Harper

I stop outside the lobby door and try to pull myself together. There are cameras inside. There are people watching me but I can't stay outside in the cold and I don't have a car. I swipe my card and head inside, my knees wobbling as I walk. I enter my office and shut the door, as if that offers privacy, but it's all I have. The tears explode from me the second I draw another breath. The tears that I cried six years ago. The tears that I have cried randomly since my miscarriage, and I wanted to call Eric every one of those teary nights. I don't know how long I cry now, but I can't stop. It guts me, it cuts me, it tears me into pieces. He's gone. Isaac told him and he's gone. My phone rings and I reach into my pocket, praying it's Eric but it's my mother. I disconnect the line and try to call Eric. He doesn't answer. I try again. And again. I cry some more.

I'm on the floor crying when I finally come back to reality. I'm on my back, staring at the ceiling. I'm hurting in every possible way. I should have told him last night. I should have told him six years ago. I force myself to my feet and I do what I have done every time I've tried to survive this. I go to my desk and try to work. I'll find out what that damn sequence is. I'll find answers and somehow that will make this better, somehow that will make Eric forgive me. No, he won't forgive me. He believes Isaac. He thinks I fucked his brother.

I dial him again and when he doesn't answer, I burst into my confession on his voicemail. "I wanted to tell you. I just didn't want you to think I was playing you and then you got rich and I was afraid you'd think it was about money. I can't make you believe me, but you know—I'm pretty sure I'm in love with you so I just have to tell you." The phone beeps and disconnects. I let out a sound of utter frustration. God. No. I need to say this.

I dial the phone again and when the machine answers I pick up where I left off. "I got pregnant the night we were together six years ago. I know you pulled out, but you were inside me and it happened. I wasn't with anyone else. I didn't think you'd believe me and what would forcing you to believe me, achieve? It was too late to change what happened. I lost the baby." The machine beeps again and I redial, my hand shaking as I do. The machine beeps again and I launch into the rest of the story. "When I missed my period, I thought it was stress, but then one night I was working late and suddenly I was bleeding. Lots of blood and Isaac was here and I was bad. I was hemorrhaging and—I had to let him help me. I didn't even know what was happening. I was scared and when I found out there was a baby—" The machine beeps. I sob with the pain of doing it like this, with reliving this. I dial again. "Bottom line," I say when I can speak again. "I hated so much that Isaac was the one who helped me. And I really wanted that baby, our baby, but now I'm damaged goods anyway. I don't even know now if I can have kids. They said—"

The machine beeps and tears stream down my cheeks. I can barely take this but I started it. I have to finish. I dial again and this time the call goes straight to voicemail. Eric turned off his phone. Obviously, he's tired of me calling. I force the words out. I start talking again. "Eric," I whisper. "I didn't betray you like everyone else in this family. Have Blake hack my medical records. If I was with Isaac and he was the father, why would I fight the ER staff and insist that I couldn't be pregnant? Why wouldn't I put him down on the medical records? I just—I need you to know that I didn't betray you. You matter to me. You've always mattered to me and I regret that I didn't call you. I regret—"

The line beeps and I add, "So much," even though he can't hear me. My emotions overflow and I throw my phone, pain behind the force that smashes it against my door. My emotions are suffocating me. I can't take it.

I stand up, not sure where I'm going, but I need to occupy my mind. I need to escape this feeling. I need to escape the pain. The sequence, I tell myself. Think about it. Think about the message. Figure out what it means. I start walking, exiting my office and walking toward the human resources office. I enter the dark office and search through files, looking for a clue. An hour later, I have nothing. I stand up again and walk toward the warehouse. That sequence has to relate to production in some way. I enter the warehouse that is now empty, as we don't run winter night shifts.

I start walking the assembly lines, looking for that fourteen-digit sequence, checking every possible place: on the parts, on the vehicles, in the paperwork at each station. I'm at this for a good half hour when I decide the foreman's office is where I need to be. I hurry that direction and I'm about to enter his office when the lights go out. I freeze in the utter, complete darkness, sucking in a breath, and willing myself to remain calm. It's a power outage. Nothing more. I reach for my purse that's in my office with my destroyed phone.

A sound, a tiny sound, jolts me. Someone is here. There is a whisper in the air. Someone is right beside me. I launch myself forward to run, but it's too late. Someone grabs me from behind.

The end... for now

Thank you so much for picking up THE BASTARD! Harper and Eric's story continues very soon in THE PRINCESS— available for pre-order on all platforms now!

PRE-ORDER HERE: http://filthytrilogy.lisareneejones.com

Don't forget, if you want to be the first to know about upcoming books, giveaways, sales and any other exciting news I have to share please be sure you're signed up for my newsletter! As an added bonus every receives a free ebook when they sign-up!

http://lisareneejones.com/newsletter-sign-up/

MY NEXT RELEASE!

Cat and Reese from DIRTY RICH ONE NIGHT STAND are back in their second book and life is about to get a lot crazier in their world! Learn more here:

https://dirtyrich.weebly.com/dirty-rich-one-night-stand.html

WANT MORE LISA RENEE JONES ROMANCE?

Have you read my Dirty Rich series? A series of super sexy lawyers filled with passion and mystery! Check it out here:

http://dirtyrich.lisareneejones.com

NEW STANDALONE COMING IN MY LILAH LOVE SERIES!

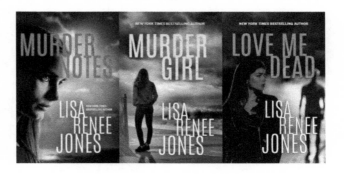

This series is a suspense series with a steamy side of romance! The first two books are available now, but the third book can be read as a standalone as well!

https://www.lilahlove.com/

A NEW PSYCHOLOGICAL THRILLER COMING SOON!

A PERFECT LIE is definitely far and away from what I usually write, but I am so excited about it! I hope you'll check it out!

https://aperfectliebook.weebly.com

ALSO BY LISA RENEE JONES

THE INSIDE OUT SERIES

If I Were You
Being Me
Revealing Us
His Secrets*
Rebecca's Lost Journals
The Master Undone*
My Hunger*
No In Between
My Control*
I Belong to You
All of Me*

THE SECRET LIFE OF AMY BENSEN

Escaping Reality
Infinite Possibilities
Forsaken
Unbroken*

CARELESS WHISPERS

Denial
Demand
Surrender

WHITE LIES

Provocative
Shameless

TALL, DARK & DEADLY

Hot Secrets
Dangerous Secrets
Beneath the Secrets

WALKER SECURITY

Deep Under
Pulled Under
Falling Under

LILAH LOVE

Murder Notes
Murder Girl
Love Me Dead (March 2019)

DIRTY RICH

Dirty Rich One Night Stand
Dirty Rich Cinderella Story
Dirty Rich Obsession
Dirty Rich Betrayal
Dirty Rich Cinderella Story: Ever After
Dirty Rich One Night Stand: Two Years Later (Dec. 2018)
Dirty Rich Obsession: All Mine (Jan. 2019)

THE FILTHY TRILOGY

The Bastard
The Princess
The Empire

*eBook only

ABOUT THE AUTHOR

New York Times and USA Today bestselling author Lisa Renee Jones is the author of the highly acclaimed INSIDE OUT series.

In addition to the success of Lisa's INSIDE OUT series, she has published many successful titles. The TALL, DARK AND DEADLY series and THE SECRET LIFE OF AMY BENSEN series, both spent several months on a combination of the New York Times and USA Today bestselling lists. Lisa is also the author of the bestselling the bestselling LILAH LOVE and WHITE LIES series.

Prior to publishing, Lisa owned a multi-state staffing agency that was recognized many times by The Austin Business Journal and also praised by the Dallas Women's Magazine. In 1998 Lisa was listed as the #7 growing women owned business in Entrepreneur Magazine.

Lisa loves to hear from her readers. You can reach her on Twitter and Facebook daily.

CPSIA information can be obtained
at www.ICGtesting.com
Printed in the USA
LVHW041952060219
606614LV00001B/29/P